Praise for *The Dirt Diary*

"Holy fried onion rings! Fun from beginning to end."
— Wendy Mass, *New York Times* bestselling author
of *11 Birthdays* and *The Candymakers*

"I LOVED it...sweet, sensitive, and delicious!"
— Erin Dionne, author of
Models Don't Eat Chocolate Cookies

"It's laugh-out-loud funny and one of the most fun books
I've read all year."

— *Justine* magazine

"Confidently addressing a number of common tween
troubles that include bullying, parental divorce, and peer
pressure, Staniszewski introduces a determined eighth
grader desperate to get her separated parents back together
in this humorous problem novel."

— *Publishers Weekly*

Praise for *The Prank List*

"*The Prank List* hooks readers with snappy dialogue from the beginning... Rachel is a likable character for middle school readers, who will relate to her problems."

—*VOYA*

"Staniszewski keeps the focus on comedy...but she lets her story become a bit more serious with the pranks Rachel plays... Gentle fun laced with equally gentle wisdom."

—*Kirkus Reviews*

"Tween readers who find Rachel endearing will find a fast-paced comedy of errors."

—*School Library Journal*

Praise for *I'm With Cupid*

"Readers are in for a wild and hilarious ride from upcoming installments in the Switched at First Kiss series."

—*Booklist*

"A cute twist on *Freaky Friday*...a great romance story for tweens and teens who want something lighthearted, fun, and magical."

—*San Francisco Book Review*

"A cute and mild love story with a dash of supernatural charm that dives a little deeper with its exploration of death and love."

—*School Library Journal*

"As always, Staniszewski provides a deft mix of comedy and sensitive, deeper themes, making her book not only entertaining, but one that offers wisdom."

—*Kirkus Reviews*

the truth game

Also by
Anna Staniszewski

The Dirt Diary Series
The Dirt Diary

The Prank List

The Gossip File

Switched at First Kiss Series
I'm With Cupid

Finders Reapers

My Very UnFairy Tale Life Series
My Very UnFairy Tale Life

My Epic Fairy Tale Fail

My Sort of Fairy Tale Ending

the truth game

ANNA STANISZEWSKI

sourcebooks
jabberwocky

Copyright © 2016 by Anna Staniszewski
Cover and internal design © 2016 by Sourcebooks, Inc.
Series design by Regina Flath
Cover image © Michael Heath/Shannon and Associates

Sourcebooks and the colophon are registered trademarks of Sourcebooks, Inc.

Published by Sourcebooks Jabberwocky, an imprint of Sourcebooks, Inc.
P.O. Box 4410, Naperville, Illinois 60567-4410
(630) 961-3900
Fax: (630) 961-2168
www.sourcebooks.com

Library of Congress Cataloging-in-Publication data is on file with the publisher.

Source of Production: Versa Press, East Peoria, Illinois, USA
Date of Production: March 2016
Run Number: 5006162

Printed and bound in the United States of America.
VP 10 9 8 7 6 5 4 3 2 1

For anyone who's ever made a huge mess.

Chapter 1

Rachel, what could possibly be taking so long?" Mom calls, banging on the bathroom door. "Do you want to be late for school?"

"I'll be right out!" I try to wrangle my hair into a bun one more time, but it's hopeless. Nothing can cover up the disaster springing out of my scalp.

Mom's pounding comes again. "You'll miss the bus!"

Ugh. Why did I think putting my hair in small braids for the night would make it look good? The genetic lottery gave me all of my dad's thick, black mane and none of my mom's blond waves, so the braids only succeeded in putting a million zigzag creases into my hair. I don't think a poodle could pull off this look. And even worse, because my hair is sticking up all over the place, the widow's peak that I'm always trying to hide is now on full display.

With a sigh, I open the door. When Mom sees me, she

starts giggling. Great. You know you look ridiculous when the one person who's always supposed to support you laughs in your face.

"Mom, what am I supposed to do? I look like I ran my head through a car wash."

Maybe I should take a page from my best friend Marisol's book and plop a tiara on my head to distract from my hair disaster. She did that last year to take attention away from a huge zit on her chin. But I have a feeling even a tiara won't help me now.

When she finally stops tittering, Mom gets a thoughtful look. Then, in full Ms. Fix-It mode, she takes my hand and pulls me over to the sink. "Dunk your head under," she says, turning on the tap.

"What about the bus?"

"I'll drive you," she says. "But we have to hurry."

There's no time to wait for the water to heat up, so I shove my head under the cold stream and close my eyes. So much for starting high school on the right note. On top of the hair fiasco, I also accidentally globbed toothpaste on my lucky shirt and somehow misplaced one of my shoes.

When my hair is soaked through, I quickly towel it off and rush to change my shirt and throw on a pair of worn-out sneakers that probably should have gone in the trash months ago. When I glance at myself in the mirror, I groan.

Oh my goldfish. I look worse than my usual self, not better! But it's too late to do anything about it. I grab a banana and my backpack and dash to meet my mom at her dented minivan, which is loaded up for her day of cleaning houses.

"Why would you do that to your beautiful hair in the first place?" Mom asks as we speed off toward the school. The mops and brooms in the back of the car bang together with every turn.

I shrug, embarrassed to admit that I had imagined myself stepping into the high school for the first time as the new and improved version of myself. After the summer I've had—working for my mom's cleaning business, running baking competitions, and dealing with all sorts of family drama—I feel like a totally different person than I did last spring. I guess I wanted to look like one too.

"Was it to impress Evan?" Mom adds with a smile.

Okay, it doesn't hurt that my boyfriend—my *boyfriend*!—is going to be at my school this year. His dad lost his job a few weeks ago, which means that the private

3

school for geniuses where Evan had been going is no longer an option—at least for now. I know Evan was bummed about having to change schools, but I'm selfishly glad that I'll get to see him every day and show him off to everyone.

There's another reason I was hoping to make myself look better than normal today. I wanted to get my mind off the fact that, for the first time in my life, my dad isn't here on my first day of school. There's no silly joke from him at breakfast or funny note from him in my lunch. Ever since my parents split up six months ago, Dad's been in Florida, and even though he's been talking about moving back home, it's probably not going to happen anytime soon.

"Oh!" Mom says as we pull onto Main Street. "Isn't today the day you find out about *Pastry Wars*?"

I groan. "Didn't we say we weren't going to talk about that? I don't want to jinx anything."

She laughs. "Sorry! I'm just so excited! I know you'll get in for sure. Your audition video was adorable."

I almost died a few weeks ago when I found out that my favorite show, *Pastry Wars*, was holding auditions for a teen episode. Of course I had to send in a video, and since my fashion-designer best friend made me look amazing and her filmmaker boyfriend shot the whole thing, I'd like to think my chances of being picked are pretty good. I bet not a lot of the other kids made super-fancy French desserts for their auditions.

"Okay, I won't bring it up again," Mom says, "but I'll be keeping my fingers crossed all day! Wouldn't it be wild if we actually got to meet Chip?"

Mom has recently developed a huge celebrity crush on *Pastry Wars* host Chip Ackerson. You'd think her boyfriend, Mr. Hammond, would be jealous, but he finds it hilarious that she acts like she and Chip are old friends when she's never even seen him in real life. But maybe that will change. Fingers, toes, and eyes crossed.

It might seem crazy that painfully shy me would be excited about being on TV, but if I'm really going to be a pastry chef one day, then I can't imagine a better way to show everyone how serious I am than by winning a major Cooking Network competition. Besides, shy me was middle school Rachel. High school is a fresh start, and I'm determined to finally leave my loser-ish reputation behind. If only the thought of finding my way through that huge building filled with strangers didn't make my whole body—even my elbows—quiver!

We turn into the school driveway, and Mom suddenly

starts sniffling. "I remember when you were a little bundle in my arms, no bigger than a loaf of bread. And now you're getting so grown up!"

Oh boy. Thankfully, we pull up to the school before Mom can start crying. "Thanks for the ride!" I say as I give her a quick peck on the cheek and then rush out of the car.

"Have fun today!" she calls after me. "Don't forget to floss after lunch!"

I practically run toward the entrance, hoping no one heard her. But I make it only a few steps before I spot Angela Bareli leaning against the flagpole in front of the school steps. I haven't seen her in over a month, and the last time was right after she'd confessed to stealing a necklace and blaming it on me. Even though her clothes and hair look the same as usual, there's something about her that seems completely different. It takes me a second to realize what it is. She's smiling—genuinely smiling—for the first time in…well, maybe in forever. And she's surrounded by a group of kids I've never seen before.

"Rachel Lee!" she says, waving me over. "How was your summer?"

"Um, it was good," I say, eyeing the small crowd around her. Unlike my middle school, the high school is regional, so half the kids are from the neighboring town. That's probably why I don't recognize any of these girls. "How about you?"

"Fantastic," she says. "Have you met my cross-country friends? We've been training like crazy for the past couple of weeks. It's going to be an amazing season."

An older-looking girl with spiked black hair gives Angela a bright smile. "Definitely," she says. "I'm the captain this year, and Angela's one of our star freshmen. She says she's never run before, but she's a natural."

"Wow," I say, and it's not because I'm impressed by Angela's running skills. For as long as I've known her, Angela Bareli has been a total follower, flocking after the popular kids, desperate to be accepted. But now, finally, she seems to have found people she actually fits with. Hopefully, when I go to the school's Cooking Club meeting this week, I'll find my people too.

Suddenly, Angela's eyes double in size. "Um, Rachel?" she whispers. "Not to freak you out or anything, but I can kind of see your bra."

I glance down and gasp. Oh my goldfish! My wet hair soaked through my T-shirt and now the fabric is practically transparent. I yank a sweatshirt out of my bag and throw it on, my cheeks burning hotter than the late August sun.

Shockingly, Angela doesn't laugh at me the way she would have even a few weeks ago. Instead, she gives me a reassuring smile and whispers, "Don't worry. I don't think anyone else noticed."

Clearly, Angela's got the whole "starting high school off on a good note" thing down. And she didn't have to suffer any wardrobe or hair malfunctions to get there.

I mumble a thank-you and then rush up the front steps, hoping to get inside without any other mishaps. If I can find Evan and Marisol, everything will be okay.

But as I'm about to dart through the door, I hear an all-too-familiar voice call my name. "Rachel!"

I gasp and spin around, sure I must be hallucinating. But it's true. My dad—my *dad*!—is there on the front steps, waving at me.

"What are you doing here?" I ask after I can tear myself away from hugging him. We saw each other a few weeks ago when I went down to Florida, but having him here, at home, in front of my new school, is totally surreal.

"I wanted to surprise you!" Dad says. "I couldn't let my Rachel Roo head off for her first day without me, could I?"

He holds out a little-kid lunch box. "PB&J with a sprig of mint, just like you asked me to make you in first grade. Do you remember? I should have known back then that you were a budding chef."

It dawns on me that kids around us are staring. It's great to see my dad, of course, but this is not exactly helping me shed my loser reputation.

"Um, thanks," I say, shoving the lunch into my bag and then pulling Dad away from the doorway so that we're not in sight of every person who passes by. "Are you back for good?"

"Yup," he says. "I'm staying in a hotel for the moment, but I'm hoping to find an apartment soon."

I can't believe it. My dad is really home! Okay, so the fact that he's living in a hotel is a little weird, but now that my parents are officially split up and my mom is dating someone else, I guess it would be even weirder if he stayed at our house.

"So…" Dad says, glancing around. "Where's this boyfriend of yours? I never had a chance to talk to him at the Bake-Off."

A bell rings, making me jump. Uh-oh. Is that the homeroom bell? "Dad, I have to go. I don't want to be late."

"Let's meet here after school, okay?" he says, giving

my shoulder a squeeze. "We can go to Molly's. I've been dreaming about their ice cream for months!"

"Today? I told you I got a job at Ryan's Bakery, right? Training starts this afternoon." I was beyond excited when Chef Ryan, the toughest critic I know, called last week to offer me a job at his bakery. For a few hours a week, I'll be ringing up customers and helping out with some of the grunt work for the bakery's catering jobs. Not exactly glamorous, but it's one huge step closer to making my dream of becoming a pastry chef come true. And if I have my way, I'll be assisting Chef Ryan with the cakes and pastries in no time.

Dad's face falls. "Oh, of course. I should have known you'd have plans. No worries." He lets out a soft laugh. "We'll get together another day, okay?"

"Maybe…maybe you could come over for dinner or something this week. I'm sure Mom wouldn't mind." As I say the words, I realize that I have no idea if they're true. Mom and Dad have barely been in the same room together since they split up. I'm not sure how she'd feel about him setting foot in our house again after everything.

"We'll figure it out," he says. "Now, off you go. I don't want you getting in trouble because of me."

I give my dad a quick hug and rush away. As I go down the nearly empty hallway, I realize I have no idea where my homeroom is or where to find my locker. So much for starting high school off as the best version of myself. At this rate, I'll be lucky to start high school on *any* note.

Chapter 2

The morning is a blur of total strangers, thick textbooks, and mazelike hallways. I can't believe how ginormous this school is and how old all the upperclassmen look. Some of the guys even have beards! Like, bushy mountain-man ones! And I actually mistook a senior girl for my math teacher. Luckily, I figured out my mistake before she assigned me any homework. Still, I've never felt so young and so totally lost.

By the time lunch rolls around, I'm desperate to see my best friend, Marisol. When we compared our schedules last week, we were horrified to learn that we'd only get to see each other during lunch. Evan's in all the supersmart classes, so his schedule is totally different from mine too, but we do have one class together—gym, of all things. Weirdly, Angela Bareli has been in all my classes so far. Whoever made the class schedules was clearly out to get me.

When I spot Marisol at a table in the corner by herself, I sprint over. "I'm so glad I found you! I was afraid I'd have to eat lunch by myself." I actually had nightmares last night about wandering the cafeteria alone for an eternity, not knowing where to sit or where to dispose of my lunch tray.

"No danger of that," she says. "Andrew's here too. He's buying lunch."

"Did you finally talk to your mom about letting you date him?" I ask.

She sighs and shakes her head. I guess when your mom is convinced you're too young for a boyfriend, it doesn't matter how sweet and harmless the guy is.

"But you finally told Andrew that your mom still doesn't know you two are together, right?"

Her cheeks grow pink. "I keep trying, but I don't want to hurt his feelings. Anyway, I'm sure my mom will come around soon, and then it won't matter." She starts intently studying her sandwich.

She clearly doesn't want to talk about it anymore, so I ask, "How's the first day going so far?"

"Great! Andrew met me at my locker this morning, and he's been walking me to all of my classes. Isn't that sweet?"

"Are boyfriends supposed to do stuff like that?" I ask,

realizing I've never paid attention to that kind of thing before. Should Evan have offered to walk me to classes, or was that something we were supposed to do automatically? So far, I'd only seen him from afar after second period. We waved to each other from across the lobby as I rushed off to figure out where my locker was. Apparently, this whole "having a boyfriend at my school" thing is going to take some getting used to.

"I tried to find you before homeroom," Marisol says. "Were you running late?"

"Sort of." I start to tell her about my disastrous morning, but I realize that she's not really listening. She's scanning the cafeteria as if she's looking for someone better to talk to. "And then I turned into an elephant and flew away, using my huge ears as wings," I finish.

"Cool," she says, glancing over her shoulder. Then she blinks, as if realizing what I said. "Wait, what? Sorry! I'm trying to find Ms. Emerald."

"Er, is that a fortune-telling cat or something?" I ask.

Marisol laughs. "No, it's a person. She's the teacher you go to if you want to start a new club. I've heard that if you can get in good with her, she'll agree to be the adviser for just about anything."

"Is that why you're so decked out?" I ask, scanning Marisol's outfit. She's practically blinding in her bright-yellow skirt, shimmery red shirt, and blue cowboy boots. On anyone else, the outfit would look ridiculous, but Marisol manages to pull it off. It probably helps that she's one of the most confident people I know.

"I have to make a good impression," she says. "If I'm going to start a fashion club, I have to look like I know what I'm talking about. Are you going to the Cooking Club meeting tomorrow?"

"Any chance I could convince you to come with me?"

Marisol lets out a honking laugh. "Only if you want me to accidentally burn the entire school down. How about you stick to baking and I'll stick to sewing, okay? The world will be a much safer place that way."

I guess I'll have to brave the Cooking Club meeting on my own. But hey, if I'm really trying to get on TV, then I guess I better get used to meeting tons of strangers. Besides, the Cooking Club will be a great chance for me to push myself to try new recipes. Between that and my job at the bakery, I'll be a pro in no time.

Andrew Ivanoff shuffles over to our table and plops down next to Marisol, giving me an awkward wave hello.

Considering that Andrew's the shyest guy I know, it's kind of a miracle that he and Marisol managed to find each other. In a weird way, I actually helped them since the complete mess I made at the end of eighth grade brought them together.

Andrew looks down at his lunch tray and frowns, poking at what could be a brick of Play-Doh with his fork.

"Doesn't look too appetizing, does it?" I ask, suddenly glad my dad brought me lunch this morning. Since I didn't know what was socially acceptable in high school, I figured buying lunch was the safer bet. But it looks like most kids bring theirs anyway, even though they put them in bags and not dorky lunch boxes.

"Actually," Andrew says, "I was wondering if it would be interesting to do a documentary on cafeteria food."

Marisol and I exchange a look. Ever since Andrew went to film camp over the summer, he's started taking the whole filmmaking thing a lot more seriously. Instead of making hilarious zombie flicks using decapitated Barbies, now he keeps looking for "real life" things to film. So far he's considered doing documentaries on life in the suburbs, an in-depth look at lawn care, and an exposé on dental floss. Marisol and I have managed to gently steer him away from all of those snooze-worthy topics, but I'm not sure how much longer we'll be able to keep it up.

"You'll never guess who I saw this morning," I say, trying to change the topic. Then I tell them about my dad surprising me on the school steps.

"You mean he's back for good this time?" Marisol says. "That's great! But it must be kind of weird too, right?"

"Kind of," I admit. Of course I'm glad Dad is back. It's what I've been dreaming of for months. But seeing him at school this morning, so totally out of context, made me realize how much has changed since he left. In a way, it feels like we're starting all over. My first instinct is to freak out about how different things are going to be, but I remind myself that I'm not the same Rachel who went a little crazy last spring and stole money from my college fund to try to go down to Florida and talk Dad into coming home. I'm new and improved Rachel now, and that means I can handle anything.

• • •

I never thought I'd look forward to gym class, but it means I'll finally have a chance to see Evan. Since it's the first day, the teacher makes us watch an ancient safety video starring an old guy who looks like a horse. Evan manages to sit next to me on the bleachers as we get ready to watch, and when he puts his hand by his side, I realize it's only an inch away from mine.

I glance around, sure everyone is staring at us. I mean, look at us. We're almost holding hands! In gym class! But the other kids are all busy snickering as Horse Guy starts talking about "avoiding charley horses" and "the dangers of horseplay." Do the gym teachers actually expect us to take this video seriously?

When class is over, Evan turns to me with a bright smile. "How's your day going so far, Booger Crap?"

I should be mortified that he'd call me that goofy nickname in public, especially since it's based on one of my dad's silly fake swears, but I can't help feeling giddy that my boyfriend—my *boyfriend*!—is sitting right next to me in school. I wish Briana and Caitlin and all the other kids who made my life miserable last year were here to see this, so I could prove to them once and for all that I am not a loser.

"Good," I say. "Good. Are you good? Because I'm good." Okay. Maybe I'm still a tiny bit of a loser.

Luckily, Evan seems to find my total awkwardness endearing. "Good," he says with his trademark crooked grin. "Where's your next class?"

After comparing schedules, we realize that our next classes are on opposite sides of the school. We might as well be freshmen on totally different continents. So much for walking each other to class.

"Well," Evan says as we lurk outside the gym, "I guess I'll see you later."

"Um, yeah. I'm working at the bakery after school, but I'll call you when I get home?"

"Sounds good."

We stand for a long, awkward moment, and I wonder if he's going to kiss me right here in front of the gym. So far our relationship has been mostly hand-holding and a few sweet pecks on the cheek, but I know the First Real Kiss is coming soon. I totally messed it up when Evan saw me off at the airport a few weeks ago, and we haven't had a chance to recreate the perfect moment since I've been back. Maybe I need to signal to Evan that I'm ready to try the kiss again.

So even though we're surrounded by the smell of floor wax and smelly sneakers, I flash him an encouraging smile. Then, just in case, I gaze deeply into his eyes and try to give him an "I'm ready to kiss you" look.

"Are you okay?" Evan asks after a second. "Your eye is twitching."

"What? Oh, I'm fine." So much for that idea.

The warning bell rings, and Evan flashes me another crooked grin. "Well, see ya," he says. Then he hurries off to catch up with a couple of guy friends, and I turn to walk the confusing hallways by myself.

Chapter 3

After school, I show up at Ryan's Bakery exactly on time. When I took a pastry class here over the summer, Chef Ryan pretty much hated my guts. It took me weeks to prove myself to him, and I'm determined to stay on his good side. I take a deep breath and paste a smile on my face, one that I hope screams, "Look at me! I'm the perfect employee!"

But when I go into the bakery, my smile fades as I spot the embodiment of pure evil, Briana Riley—Evan's twin sister—lurking by the counter. Except she's not *by* the counter, she's *behind* it, and she's wearing an apron with a Ryan's Bakery logo on it. As if she works here. What the Shrek? That's impossible. Briana Riley would never stoop so low.

The minute she spots me, her cheeks turn pink. Clearly, she's mortified that I've seen her.

"What are you doing here?" I ask.

"None of your business," she spits out. "Are you going to buy something, or what?"

"No. I mean, no. I mean, I work here now. Too. Like you do." Yeah, I've never been at my most articulate around Briana. She has the power to bring me to tears with one of her snide remarks. But I know she's not nearly as strong as she pretends to be. I saw the cracks in her armor last year when her best friend, Caitlin Schubert, and her boyfriend, Steve Mueller, both dumped her (even though the three of them have patched things up since then). Briana doesn't scare me anymore, I remind myself.

"You're the other cashier?" she says in disbelief. "Chef Ryan said it was someone who knew what they were doing."

"I do know what I'm doing. I worked at a café over the summer." I don't mention that it was only for a week and that I practically got fired from the job because I was falsely accused of swiping cash from the register. "How come Evan didn't tell me you were working here?"

She rolls her eyes. "As if I tell my brother anything. Besides, it's not a big deal. Once my dad finds a new job, I'm totally going to quit."

But I can tell it *is* a big deal, at least to her. She's always been a spoiled princess. Last time I checked, princesses didn't work, and they definitely didn't wear aprons.

"Why are *you* here?" she adds. "I thought you were doing that whole cleaning lady thing."

"I am but only on Saturdays." Now that Mom has merged her cleaning business with the more established Ladybug Cleaners, she doesn't need me to help out as much, and she even encouraged me to take this bakery job. But maybe this was a huge mistake. How am I supposed to work side by side with Briana Riley?

Briana takes out her phone and slumps against the counter. A second later she gasps. "No way!"

"What's wrong?"

"I just found out I got a super-high score on yesterday's Truth Game questions. Like my highest yet," she says.

"What's the Truth Game?" I'm surprised the word "truth" is even in Briana's vocabulary. She's willing to say pretty much anything to make people feel like pond scum. She's certainly done it to me.

"You've seriously never heard of it?" she asks. "Everyone's playing it. It's like Truth or Dare meets Have You Ever. You own up to stuff you've done and see how your answers compare to other people's. Plus, you get bonus points for doing dares."

"Wow," I say. That sounds terrible. As if I don't already feel like people are judging me all the time.

"I got a bunch of points because I admitted that I cheated on a final exam," Briana says proudly.

"Why would you post that on the Internet? What if a teacher sees it and you get in trouble?"

"Duh," she says. "It's anonymous. No one would admit to anything if everyone knew who you were."

At that moment Chef Ryan storms in, looking annoyed as usual. "Cherie will be here in a minute to train you two. You"—he points to Briana—"package up the day-old cookies while you're waiting. Rachel, show her what to do and then come with me. I have a cake for you to work on." Then he disappears in the back again.

My heart leaps. Chef Ryan is trusting me with a cake already!

"Who's Cherie?" Briana says.

"Chef Ryan's wife. She runs the catering part of the bakery." Cherie isn't as skilled in the kitchen as her husband, but she more than makes up for it with her people skills. "The day-old cookies are over here," I say, pointing. "The bakery puts them into bags and sells them at a discount." It's a good thing I've been here a bunch of times or I'd have no idea what Chef Ryan wanted us to do.

"Wait," Briana says as I head toward the back room. "What about—?"

"Sorry," I say as Chef Ryan calls my name. "I'll be back." I'm not going to babysit Briana when I have real work to do.

When I get in the back room, Chef Ryan's waiting there with a cake that's already been half decorated with buttercream roses.

"How are your icing skills?" he asks.

"Um…" I make a lot of desserts, but I usually sprinkle them with chocolate chips or drizzle them with glaze. "I haven't had a lot of experience decorating cakes," I admit.

"That's why you're here, to learn. Okay, while I work on this, you practice on some wax paper."

"Wait, I don't actually get to ice the cake?"

"It's your first day on the job," he says. "Be glad I'm even letting you in the kitchen."

I sigh and pick up the icing bag. Then I squeeze out a rose onto some wax paper.

"Not bad," Chef Ryan says. "But try it this way." He barely flicks his wrist, and a perfect rose appears next to the one I made.

I do another flower, and it comes out a little better. By the third one, I'm actually feeling pretty good. "Are you sure I can't do any real ones?" I ask.

Chef Ryan goes back over to the cake. "After you do about a hundred of those, I'll think about it."

A hundred? Is he serious? But he just focuses on decorating the cake with one perfect flower after another, so I guess he means it.

I work on rose after rose, trying to do them as fast as possible. The more I do though, the worse they look.

"Slow down," Chef Ryan says, not even looking up from his work. He must have eyes in his ears or something.

"You know what would look really great?" I say after a minute. "Some leaves and vines around the flowers."

He studies the cake he's working on and then shakes his head. "Sometimes less is more."

But I don't have time to think like that. If I'm really going to be on *Pastry Wars*, then the bigger, the better. The girl who won the Fourth of July–themed teen show last season made a red, white, and blue velvet cake that crackled when you bit into it. She even put sparklers on top!

As I get back to making endless rows of roses, I start imagining what life will be like after I make it onto *Pastry Wars*. I'll get to meet Chip Ackerson and the judges who are usually super-important pastry chefs, and who knows, maybe one of them will like my stuff so much that he or she will offer me a job at some fancy bakery when I'm older. And if I win the show, I'll get a scholarship that I'll be able to use to help pay for culinary school one day (which is a big reason Mom was excited about me applying, besides the fact that she wants to meet Chip in person). But mostly I imagine what it's going to be like to come home a TV star, even if I don't win. No one will make fun of me for keeping a baking journal or for doing or saying the wrong thing. Once people see what I can really do, I know they'll finally take me seriously.

When my lesson is over, Chef Ryan sends me out front to help Briana. I find Cherie standing at the counter, studying a pile of empty plastic bags.

"Oh, Rachel," Cherie says. She's usually ridiculously perky, but for once she's frowning. "Briana said you told her to do the cookie bags like this?"

I realize the bags only looked empty from a distance. They actually each have a single cookie in them. "Um, no," I say. There's no way Briana is blaming her mistakes on me.

"You said to package them up," Briana says.

"Not one in each bag," I say. But when I think back, I realize I didn't actually tell her how many to put inside. I was so busy rushing off to help Chef Ryan that I guess I didn't finish explaining the directions. Oops.

Cherie sighs. "No problem. We'll simply have to redo them." And I can tell that by "we" she means me. Then her face brightens. "Anyhoo, I have to go make some phone calls. I don't want to say anything yet, but if all goes well, I'll have some great news to share soon!"

"Oh joy," Briana says, rolling her eyes. Clearly, baking news doesn't excite her, but I'm dying to know what Cherie is talking about. Before I can bombard her with questions though, she flashes us a smile and disappears into the back office.

"Okay, I guess we should open all these up and redo them," I say, grabbing a couple of the nearly empty cookie bags.

"How about you do that and I'll supervise?" Briana says.

"You don't want me to do them wrong and then blame it on you again, do you?" Then she flashes me a fake smile and goes back to tapping away on her phone.

Ugh. Once a princess, always a princess. I have no choice but to get to work.

Chapter 4

When I get home from work, Mom is waiting for me with an episode of *Pastry Wars* already queued up on the TV. After I was in a bake-off this summer, Mom got really into watching food competitions. She even recorded a bunch of episodes of *Pastry Wars* while I was in Florida so that we could watch them together. It's funny that before my dad left, Mom and I seemed so different from each other that we could barely have a conversation. Now, I feel closer to her than I do to pretty much anyone else.

"Any news yet?" she asks, and I know she means about the show.

I shake my head. "I've been checking my email all day, but nothing yet."

Mom sighs. "Okay then, talk to me," she says as we settle in on the couch and start nibbling on dinner, some leftover spinach and shallot quiche that I made the other day. "How was the first day?"

I tell her about how I spent most of it wandering around totally lost and how I barely saw Evan or Marisol or anyone else I know.

Mom pats my hand. "You'll adjust to it all soon enough. Don't worry." She picks up the TV remote. "I can't wait to watch this episode! They're supposed to make cookies that you can stack like Legos. Isn't that wild? And Chip is wearing dark blue in this one. You know how much I love him in blue!"

I swallow a bite of quiche. "And, um, Dad was there today."

She looks at me. "At your school?"

"He brought me lunch this morning, said he didn't want to miss my first day." Her reaction means she had no idea he was back in town. I shouldn't be too surprised. Knowing Dad, he probably decided to move and had his bags packed and his plane ticket booked all in the span of a day. He's always been kind of impulsive that way.

"Well," Mom says. "Well." Clearly, she's a little stunned. I guess she didn't really believe that he would come back either. At least not so soon. Maybe Dad's trying to reinvent himself like I am.

Then my phone tells me I have a new email, and I forget all about my dad. All I can do is stare at the email titled: "Your *Pastry Wars: Teen Edition* Application." Oh my goldfish. It's here!

"Open it, open it, open it," Mom chants when I tell her.

Finally, with shaking hands, I open the email and start reading.

Dear applicant,

Thank you for your interest in being on *Pastry Wars: Teen Edition.* While we think you have a lot of talent, we cannot offer you a spot on this season's show. We wish you the best of luck in your baking endeavors, and we encourage you to try again next year!

Sincerely,

Chip Ackerson and the *Pastry Wars* Team

The phone slips out of my hands and drops on the couch. "I didn't get in," I say softly.

"What? That's impossible!" Mom says. She reads the email, and her frown lines get deeper and deeper. "Oh, honey. I'm sorry."

I know I'm being stupid. Getting onto the show was a long shot. It was like setting my heart on winning the lottery or something. But I can't help it. I did set my heart on it, and now my heart's been crushed.

● ● ●

It's an annual tradition for Marisol and me to rehash every minute of our first day of school over the phone on the first night. Last year, I remember gushing about Steve Mueller for about half the conversation while Marisol considered what outfit she should wear the next day. This year, I'm obsessing about getting rejected from *Pastry Wars* while Marisol stresses about Ms. Emerald not wanting to advise the Fashion Club.

"I can't believe she said she doesn't know enough about fashion!" Marisol says on the other end. "You should have seen her shoes. They were straight out of a magazine!"

"Maybe she just doesn't want to do it." I can't blame someone for not being a club joiner. The only club I'd ever consider is the cooking one. Nothing else sounds at all exciting.

"But she has to," Marisol insists. "All the other teachers are already advising clubs or coaching sports teams. I asked the guidance counselor about it, and he said she's the only one left."

It figures that we've been in school for only a day, and Marisol has already talked to the guidance counselor. When she's focused on a goal, she doesn't waste any time. Somehow that only makes me feel worse about not being on *Pastry Wars*. Marisol has her life all planned out, and just when I thought I did too, it all fell apart.

"The outfit you made for my audition video was perfect," I tell Marisol. "You should show it to Ms. Emerald."

She lets out a breath into the phone. "I still don't get why they didn't pick you, especially since your dessert was so fancy! I've never seen you make anything like that before."

After days of rejecting recipes, I'd finally decided on a mille-feuille, which is a three-layered cake with pastry cream, whipped cream, and frosting smeared in between layers of puff pastry. I figured an ooh-la-la French pastry would definitely wow everyone. I guess I was wrong.

"If you want, I could bake something for Ms. Emerald," I offer. "Food bribery always does the trick."

I hear Marisol giggle. "I'm not sure that would prove to her that I should have a *fashion* club. Andrew said he could make a film to help me plead my case, but he's so wrapped up in his new school lunch documentary that I doubt he'll have time."

We groan in unison. Andrew ignored our advice and went ahead with the school lunch idea. I'm hoping he'll put a couple of zombie toys in it and liven things up, but so far, he's been really focused on getting exclusive interviews with the lunch ladies. They've been doing their best to avoid him.

"Hopefully, he'll figure out a different topic," I say. Talking about Marisol's boyfriend makes me think about Evan. "So...I had a question. How do you know when to hold Andrew's hand? Do you grab it every time you see him?"

"I don't know," Marisol says, her voice dropping to a whisper the way it does whenever she talks about things with Andrew, just in case her mom is nearby. "I guess I hold it whenever it feels right."

"But how do you know it's right? Is there a signal he

gives you or something? Like what if Evan wants to hold my hand before gym class, but I totally miss the signal?"

"Rachel, you're overthinking this. There's no right or wrong way."

That's easy for her to say. She's obviously doing it the right way without even realizing it. But maybe she's right and I am overthinking things.

"Okay, I'll stop stressing about it," I tell her. "I guess I'm just—"

"Hold on a sec," Marisol says. Then I hear muffled voices in the background. "Sorry," she says after a second. "My mom's reminding me it's a school night, and I still have to go through my outfits and figure out which ones to bring for Ms. Emerald tomorrow. I'll talk to you later, okay?"

Then she hangs up the phone, and I realize that it's the first time we've ended our first-night-of-school conversation without doing our yearly prayer to the pineapple gods. A few years ago, we'd both had way too much sugar and were dancing around my kitchen with a couple of pineapples. (Don't ask.) Somehow that led to us begging the pineapple gods to help make our school years amazing, and the tradition stuck. Yes, it's kind of bizarre, but when you're really low on the popularity totem pole, sometimes you get a little desperate.

Even though Marisol already hung up, I hold the phone to my chest like we always do. Then I close my eyes and whisper, "I call on the pineapple gods to hear my prayer. Please, let me be the best version of myself this year. And please, please, please, let my desserts get on TV somehow!" Then I bow my head and add, "Praise be to your delicious tropical juices."

When I open my eyes, for just a second, I get a little tingle down my spine. And that's when I know for sure that the pineapple gods have heard me.

Chapter 5

E van," Andrew suddenly says through a mouthful of
mashed potatoes at lunch the next day.

"What?" I say.

"Evan," he says again, motioning toward the front of
the cafeteria.

I turn to find Evan waving at me from the doorway.
What is he doing here? I jump up and hurry over to meet
him. "Aren't you supposed to be in Spanish class?"

He holds up a bathroom pass. "It's down the hall, so I
thought I'd say hi and see how you're holding up."

I have the urge to throw my arms around him. "Still
bummed about *Pastry Wars*," I admit, "but better now that
you're here."

He grins. "It's nice seeing you outside of gym class.
It stinks that the only time we see each other is when I
actually stink." He chuckles. "By the way, that was a nice
volleyball to the head you took today."

"Thanks. I'm really talented like that. Wait until we play basketball. I'll have a concussion in no time." I go to playfully smack his arm the way I've seen other couples do, but instead I wind up hitting him square in the elbow.

"Ow!" he cries, cradling his arm.

"Oh my goldfish. Are you okay?"

"Wow, you got my funny bone." He laughs. "You really are talented."

"I'm so sorry!" I cry, mortified, but Evan is smiling.

He shakes out his arm and then glances over his shoulder, like he's afraid of getting caught. "So, listen, can you do me a favor? My sister finally told me about working at the bakery with you, but she swore me to secrecy." He rolls his eyes. "I know having her around isn't ideal, but…anyway you could keep an eye on her? I'm kind of worried about her."

I blink at him. "You are? Why?"

"She's been acting weird lately. I know my dad losing his job hit her hard. She's not used to my parents telling her 'no,' and now she hears it all the time."

I bite my lip to keep from saying something snide. I don't exactly feel bad for Briana, but it's sweet that Evan is worried about her. Especially since they aren't exactly close.

"And that game she's been playing," he goes on. "She's kind of become obsessed with it."

"The Truth Game?" I ask.

"Yeah. She keeps asking me all these questions about stuff that happened years ago. I don't know. It can't be good to keep rehashing all the things you did, can it?"

I shrug. "Maybe it is if the past keeps coming back to bite you in the ascot," I say, using one of my dad's favorite goofy fake swears.

"Okay, gotta go," Evan says. "But I'll try to come see you tomorrow."

"Won't your Spanish teacher mind?"

"Nah. I'll tell her I have a tiny bladder." He crinkles his eyebrows. "Any idea what the word for 'bladder' is in Spanish?"

I laugh as he flashes me one last grin before disappearing around the corner. I might not be on TV, but I certainly have the best boyfriend I could ever ask for.

● ● ●

When I get to the home ec room for the first meeting of the Cooking Club, my legs freeze up in the hallway and refuse to move. I have to remind them that I belong here. This is the only club in the entire school that I'm interested in, and it could finally be my chance to be around people who love food as much as I do. I can't let my awkwardness around strangers get in the way of that. Besides, I worked with a couple of total strangers when I was in Florida, and it was fine. Well, except for the whole "getting accused of stealing" thing.

I open the door and peer inside the room, expecting to see it bursting with fellow cooking enthusiasts. Instead, I find my gym teacher leaning on one of the linoleum counters and talking to a skinny guy in supertight jeans.

"You here for the cooking club?" Mrs. Da Silva asks.

"Um, yes?"

"I know you. You're in my third-period class, right?" she says. "Lee?"

I nod. "Rachel Lee."

"Come on in. We'll start in a second. I'm hoping we'll get a couple more."

I go inside and sink into a nearby chair. This is it? One other member and a gym teacher as our adviser? This is definitely not the bustling club I was imagining where I get to finally make high school–level stuff.

"I'm Pierre Moreau," the skinny guy says with a hint of an accent.

"Hi," I say. "You're French." Ah, yes. My sparkling conversational skills never fail.

"Thank you, Captain Obvious," he says. Then he does a little snort-laugh like he's made an awesome joke. "So what kinds of things do you cook?"

"Desserts mostly. I want to be a pastry chef one day," I say. And then, for some reason, I wind up telling him about my *Pastry Wars* audition.

"Sorry you didn't get in. What did you make for it?" he asks.

"A mill fill." I wait for him to look impressed, but instead he frowns.

"A what?" Then his eyes widen. "Oh! Do you mean a mille-feuille?" His accent is perfect, and it sounds nothing like what I said. "You can also call it a Napoleon, you know."

"Oh yeah. I know," I mumble, my cheeks getting hot. Oh my goldfish. Is that why my audition video got rejected—because I couldn't pronounce the name of my dessert right? I could kick myself in the head for being such an idiot. "What kind of cooking do you do?" I ask, trying to change the subject.

"I'm into molecular gastronomy."

"Is that like the astronomy of gases?" I blurt out.

He lets out another snort-laugh. "You're funny. No, it's a scientific approach to food. You start by looking at the chemical reactions happening during the cooking process, and then you…"

But I stop listening because at that moment the door opens, and a guy comes in. I suck in a breath when I recognize him.

"Rachel!" he says, sounding surprisingly glad to see me.

"Hey, Whit," I say, getting to my feet. I should have known Adam Whitney, a.k.a. Whit, would be here. When he and I took a pastry class together during the summer at Ryan's Bakery, he'd mentioned that he lived in the next town over. Somehow though, it hadn't occurred to me that we'd be going to the same school until now. Of course he'd be in the Cooking Club when he likes baking as much as I do. Even if he's kind of full of himself about it.

"Okay," Mrs. Da Silva says, glancing at the clock. "I guess we should get started. So a little about why I'm here. The teacher who used to advise this club retired, and the school asked me to take over. I might not know a lot about cooking, but besides physical education, I also teach health, so I know all about nutrition. I figure that's a good fit."

I try not to groan. Considering that most of my desserts

are essentially flavored sticks of butter, nutrition isn't exactly on my priority list a lot of the time.

"What are our club goals?" Pierre asks, his laptop open, his fingers poised to take notes.

Mrs. Da Silva shrugs. "That's up to you all to decide. What are you interested in, Moreau?"

"I've been experimenting a lot with foams," he says. "Last week I made a porcini mushroom foam. I want to do more of that kind of thing."

"Sounds pretty low-calorie," Mrs. Da Silva says with an approving nod. Then she turns to Whit. "How about you, Whitney? Any cooking goals?"

"My sister's kids are really picky eaters. All they ever eat is Cheetos. I want to learn to cook some stuff that they'll actually like."

"Ah, the challenge of getting young people to eat healthy," Mrs. Da Silva says.

"What happened to getting a job at a fancy bakery?" I ask him. That was pretty much all he could talk about over the summer.

Whit shrugs. "I still want to do that, but I spend so much time babysitting my nephews that I guess I've been thinking more about everyday food."

"And what about you, Lee?" Mrs. Da Silva says. "What's your goal for the year?"

Is it some kind of rule that gym teachers can only call you by your last name? "I guess I want to wow people with my desserts," I say slowly.

Mrs. Da Silva gives me an uncertain look. "Okay, but is there something specific you'd like to work on?" When I can't give her an answer, she smiles and says, "Well, let's start with something small today. How do ants on a log sound? Healthy and delicious!"

I'm convinced she's joking until she takes out some celery sticks and tells us to start slicing them into "logs." Oh my goldfish. Is this really the kind of stuff we're going to be doing? Forget high school cooking. It looks like I'm back in elementary school.

Chapter 6

Marisol's eyes practically fall out of her head at lunch the next day when I tell her I'm thinking of quitting the Cooking Club.

"I'm killing myself to start a fashion club, and you're going to quit the one club at school that's perfect for you?"

"We made ants on a log!" I cry. "And next week, Mrs. Da Silva said we're going to be making trail mix."

"I like trail mix," Andrew chimes in, not looking up from his camera, which is aimed at a piece of mystery meat. He's been taking photos of the grossest-looking items served at lunch to try to figure out what they're made out of. He's actually going to bring the mystery meat to a science lab at a local college to see if it can be identified.

"Trail mix is fine," I say, "but how can we be making it for a cooking club when you don't even *cook* anything to make it?"

"Maybe you guys will get into harder stuff later on," Marisol says, but even she sounds a little skeptical. "Or you can start a baking club instead. Maybe Ms. Emerald would be the adviser."

"I thought she wouldn't even be yours."

Marisol smiles. "I overheard her talking to another teacher about needing something to wear to her brother's wedding, so I'm going to make her a one-of-a-kind dress. Then she'll have to help me with the club. I bet I could bribe her for you too."

Starting my own club sounds even worse. What if no one wanted to join? "That's okay. I guess you're right and I should give the Cooking Club another shot. Maybe it'll get better."

"Suit yourself," Marisol says with a shrug. "I'm going to the fabric store with my mom later to get stuff for Ms. Emerald's dress. You want to come? I could really use your advice."

"I can't. I'm meeting my dad for dinner. I haven't told him about *Pastry Wars* yet." I gasp, the lightbulb in my brain suddenly glowing with an idea. "I know what you should do! You should audition for one of those fashion design TV shows. They have ones for high school kids, right? Then you won't need to start a fashion club because you'll be famous and everyone will be falling all over themselves to buy your stuff."

"They'd never pick me," Marisol says. "I don't have a good story. You know: 'Marisol was raised by wolves, but now she designs clothes with wolves on them.' That kind of cheesy thing."

"So you make one up," I say. "I basically did that, remember?" When Andrew told me that my audition video needed to be more personal, I decided to play up the whole "child of divorce" angle, talking about how food saved me, blah, blah, blah. Corny, yes, but definitely the kind of stuff reality shows eat up. Sadly, it didn't work.

"Um, Rachel?" Marisol says with a laugh. "Have you met me? Since when do I make stuff up? Face it, TV is not for me."

I have to laugh too. "Okay, well they'd love how honest and in-your-face you are," I tell Marisol, but I know she has a point. Marisol isn't into fashion because she cares about proving herself or being famous. She just loves designing clothes. I'm not banking on getting famous for my cooking either, but it certainly would go a long way in making me feel like a real chef. Too bad I totally blew my one opportunity to actually make it happen.

I take out my baking notebook and start flipping through, hoping something there will inspire me and make me feel better. But all the recipes seem so boring. I mean, chocolate chip brownies? That's something a little kid would make. I used to spend hours making up recipes and writing them down, but ever since I decided to audition for *Pastry Wars*, I haven't been able to focus on the same old recipes. I'm tired of feeling like I'm playing on the JV team. I want to finally be on varsity. If only someone would give me a chance.

● ● ●

When I get to the bakery that afternoon, Chef Ryan is on top of a precarious-looking ladder, watering small boxes of mint, rosemary, and sage above the bakery door. The fresh herbs were Cherie's idea, and they are a nice touch, but I don't think she considered how hard it would be to water them every day.

Not surprisingly, Briana isn't there yet. I keep my fingers crossed that she doesn't show up at all.

"You up for helping me make some fruit tarts later on?" Chef Ryan asks.

"Absolutely!" I say, my mood lightening. "I saw this one recipe on TV that I've wanted to try out. Instead of cream cheese you use—"

"Whoa!" He holds up his hands. "I only need help cutting up the fruit. I'll handle the rest."

"But…but I can do a lot more than cutting fruit."

"We'll get there, okay? Remember, you've got to crawl before you can walk," he says.

"Actually, my mom says I skipped crawling when I was a baby and went straight to walking."

Chef Ryan chuckles. "That explains a lot," he says. Then he disappears in the back room.

A minute later, Briana waltzes into the bakery and sits down behind the counter, staring at her phone as always. It's pretty annoying that she thinks this is what "working" looks like. I have no idea why Evan is so worried about her. She seems to be adjusting to her new life just fine.

As I start doing inventory of the pastries in the display cases, Briana lets out a triumphant hoot, still looking at her phone. I don't care about her winning some silly game, but maybe this is a way to get her talking so I can tell Evan that I at least tried to see how she was doing.

"Did you get more points?" I ask.

Briana nods. "I'm the only one who's ever talked my way out of a speeding ticket before even having a driver's license."

"Wow," I say because it's obvious that she wants me to look impressed. "So, um, people really don't know who you are on there? You can post anything and it's totally safe?"

"Obviously you don't want to post stuff that would identify you." Then she explains how the game is set up as a series of questionnaires. Every day or two, you get new questions about a different topic. Today's, for example, is driving. Then you put in your answers and see how they stack up against everyone else's.

"But why don't people lie and say they did stuff they didn't?" I ask. "If it's anonymous, no one will know either way."

"You can," she says, rolling her eyes. "But it's more fun to know how you really stack up against people. Anyway, you should try it. If I get you to sign up, I get bonus points."

Briana apparently thinks it's a done deal because she grabs my phone and starts installing the game on it. She sets me up with a username specially designed to insult me—"neat freak"—and a generic password, and then she tosses the phone back to me.

"Um, thanks," I say, about to slip the phone back into my bag. Unlike her, I intend to spend my afternoon working instead of clicking away. But Briana won't let me get off that easily.

"You have to at least do one questionnaire," she says. "Otherwise, what's the point?"

Since the bakery is empty anyway, I sigh and open the app. I scroll through a few questionnaires on things like driving and exercising and finally stop on one called "Dating." I make sure Briana isn't looking over my shoulder and then I start reading.

1. Are you dating anyone?

I can't help grinning as I select "yes."

2. Have you ever been kissed?

My cheeks get hot. I feel like I need to cover the screen with my hand as I check "no." It's certainly none of Briana's business what I've been doing (or not doing) with her brother!

3. Do you plan to be in your current relationship six months from now?

I stare at that question for a minute. Six months ago, Evan and I hadn't even met! Of course I want us to be together in six months, but who knows what will happen. It almost feels like I'll jinx things if I say yes, so I finally select "I don't know."

4. What's something people would be surprised
to know about your significant other?

I think for a second and then write, "He caught me snooping through his sister's underwear drawer, and he still wanted to date me! He's a keeper."

I smile a little to myself as I submit my answers. Then I realize that if Evan ever read that, he'd know it was about him. So much for being anonymous. But it doesn't matter. Even if Evan did see my answers, there's nothing there I'm ashamed of.

5. Dare! We dare you to kiss someone! Change
your answer in the next forty-eight hours, and
we'll give you bonus points!

I close the app with a sigh. Evan and I have been trying

to make our first kiss happen for weeks. I seriously doubt it's going to happen in the next two days.

When I glance at Briana, I find her staring out the window and wrapping her long ponytail around her hand. For a second, I can't help thinking how sad she looks. That can't be right. Briana Riley doesn't know how to feel human emotions like sadness. But maybe that's why Evan's been so worried about her.

She turns away from the window and catches me staring. "What?"

"Um, nothing," I say.

At that moment, Cherie bursts out of her office. "It's official!" she yells. "It's really happening!"

"What is?" I ask. "Is this the big news you were talking about?"

"Yes!" Cherie practically jumps up and down. "One of the weddings we're doing is going to be featured on the Cooking Network!"

I almost fall over. The Cooking Network? As in, home of *Pastry Wars*? "No way!" I squeak. "When? How? Where?" I have so many questions, I don't know where to start.

"So what?" Briana says, clearly not impressed.

"The Montelle-Brennan wedding was already going

to be exciting, but now it's going to be incredible," Cherie says.

"Wait...Montelle?" I ask, turning to Briana. "Caitlin Schubert's mom is getting married?"

Briana shrugs. "She met some rich guy like a month ago, and now they're doing this huge wedding. It's pretty gross." Of course Briana would be disgusted by the idea of her best friend's mother finding happiness.

"Ms. Montelle's daughter is the one to thank for this opportunity," Cherie chimes in. "She entered her mother in a contest, and their wedding was one of the four chosen to be highlighted in a 'Lavish Weddings' special. Isn't that incredible? We're so lucky Ms. Montelle and her fiancé decided to go with a local caterer instead of hiring some fancy out-of-town company."

I'm not surprised Caitlin would enter her mom's wedding into a contest. She's almost as into the Cooking Network as I am, at least judging by all the times I saw her watching *Pastry Wars* when I was over cleaning her house.

"And guess who's hosting the special?" Cherie goes on. "Chip Ackerson!"

I actually scream. "*Chip Ackerson?*"

"God," Briana says, covering her ears. "Relax."

"He's like… He's my idol," I say. "He…" I can't even put into words how amazing he is. He knows so much about pastries that he's like a dessert encyclopedia! A dessertopedia!

"We only have a few weeks to get everything together," Cherie says, ignoring the fact that I'm melting into goo, "so it looks like we hired you two just in time!"

Briana's eyes widen. "You're not going to have us *do* anything for the wedding, are you?"

"I was hoping Rachel could stay here and hold down the fort that day," Cherie says. "And, Briana, you'll be with me and my two daughters, setting up tables, serving food, and whatever else needs to be done."

Wait. This epic wedding is going to be on my favorite TV channel, and I'll be stuck at the bakery the whole time while Briana gets to see it all?

It's clear Briana's not happy about the arrangement either because she furiously shakes her head. "No way. I'm not doing that."

"Can't we switch?" I say. "I can be with you, and Briana can stay here?"

"I'm afraid not," Cherie says. "We need someone with experience to man the store while we're gone."

"But I'm not that experienced!" I say. "I only worked at a café for about a week this summer."

I expect Briana to flash me a smug look, but she's nodding. "Yeah, and setting up chairs is definitely not for me."

But Cherie has clearly made up her mind. "I appreciate that you want to help out with the wedding, Rachel, but I think my way makes the most sense." She turns to Briana. "Setting up for events is part of the job," Cherie says, pursing her lips. "I'm sure Chef Ryan told you that when he hired you. If you're not up for the task, I can find someone else for this position."

I expect Briana to throw down her apron and stomp out of the bakery. Instead, she lowers her eyes and mumbles, "Okay, fine."

Oh my goldfish. I don't think I've ever seen Briana Riley back down from anything. She must really need this job. I guess that means I'm stuck with her. But I don't care. The pineapple gods must have heard me after all. They're giving me a second chance, and I'm not going to let anything mess it up.

Chapter 7

When I meet Dad for dinner at Molly's after my shift at the bakery, I find him peering into the display case at the front of the café where they keep all the fancy desserts.

"What do you say, Rachel Roo? Think you could make me one of those?" he asks, pointing to a crème-filled torte on the top shelf.

"For you, anything," I say. I'm dying to tell him about my plan to convince Chip Ackerson to let me back on the show, but I don't want to jinx anything. So instead, I try to focus on how great it is to finally be back at my favorite restaurant with Dad.

As we make our way toward our usual table in the corner, I hear a familiar jolly laugh echoing nearby. I glance over to the other side of the café, and sure enough, there's Mr. Hammond, my former vice principal and my mom's new boyfriend. And with him is my mom.

Oh no. If they see us, are they going to want us to sit with them? I can't imagine anything more awkward.

"Um, Dad?" I start to say. "Maybe we should—"

But I don't get a chance to convince him to go elsewhere because just then Mom turns toward us, and her face lights up. "Rachel!" she calls, waving. Then she must spot my dad standing next to me because her smile falters. But it's too late. We have no choice but to go over.

After some stiff hellos and introductions (even though my dad and Mr. Hammond technically already met at my baking competition over the summer), the dreaded words come.

"We just sat down and haven't ordered yet," Mr. Hammond says. "Why don't you two join us?"

My dad doesn't even hesitate. "Sure! If you don't mind."

Mom gives a little nod, but I can tell she does mind. And so do I. Not only had I wanted some alone time with Dad, but I can't imagine what the four of us will talk about. You can't chitchat about the weather through a whole meal, can you?

For the first few minutes, we focus on our menus and some general talk about how great Molly's is. It flows so smoothly that I start to wonder if I was being a paranoid panther. But after we order our crepes, there's a looong silence when we're all staring at our silverware. Finally, Mr. Hammond turns to my dad and says, "Now that you're back, what are you planning to do for work, Ted?"

Dad clears his throat. "That's still a work in progress. But I'm sure something will turn up."

I can see Mom's jaw tighten. Dad's been paying child support since he left, but I know it hasn't helped out as much as she'd hoped. And now that he doesn't have a job, who knows what will happen? Thankfully, her cleaning business is doing better these days, but I know she's still pretty mad at my dad for leaving us high and dry.

"Have you been looking?" Mom asks.

"I only got back into town," Dad says, smoothing down his napkin. "I haven't had a chance yet."

"You could have tried to line something up before you came up here," she points out. "At least set up some interviews over the phone."

Dad laughs. "You know planning has never been my forte, Amanda," he says, which is probably the worst thing he could say since Mom is one of the biggest planners on the planet.

"That doesn't mean you can't try to be better at it,"

she says. "Just because we've made mistakes in the past doesn't mean we have to keep repeating them. Think about your daughter!"

Oh boy. It sounds like all the stuff Mom has been *not* saying for years is finally leaking out. I can practically hear the ground rumbling under us, the volcano about to erupt.

"I heard it's supposed to snow tomorrow," I blurt out. Of course, that's totally untrue, but I can't let this conversation keep going like this.

Mr. Hammond raises an eyebrow. "Really? This time of year?"

"I might have to ski to school!" I say. "Wouldn't that be crazy, Mom? Dad?" But they're not listening.

"Think about my daughter?" Dad repeats. "Do you think I've somehow forgotten about her? I do nothing but think about how I can make her happy. That's why I came back in the first place."

"You certainly weren't thinking about that when you left!" Mom says, her voice growing louder. People are staring at us, which is mortifying since my family has been coming here for as long as I can remember. The waitstaff knows us all, and now they're watching us have a total meltdown.

I need to do something to make it stop.

"I'm going to be on TV!" I practically yell.

My parents finally stop glaring at each other and look at me. "What was that?" Mom says.

Then, in a tumble of words, I tell them all about the Montelle-Brennan wedding. "If I can show Chip Ackerson that I deserve to be on TV, maybe he'll give me another chance at *Pastry Wars*!"

"Chip's going to be in town?" Mom asks, looking like she might swoon. "Really?" Mr. Hammond rolls his eyes, but he's smiling.

"I don't know if I'll actually be at the wedding," I admit, "but I'm sure I'll be able to find some way to get my desserts to Chip."

"That's great, Roo," Dad says, but for some reason he doesn't sound as excited as I thought he'd be.

"You don't think he should give me another chance?" I ask him.

"Of course I do! I think they were dingbats to reject you in the first place. I don't want you to get your hopes up, that's all. Things like this can be so unpredictable."

"Your father's right," Mom says, and I'm shocked to hear them agreeing on something.

"But I've been working so hard at my baking," I say.

"I'm so much better than I was a few months ago. I know if I can get Chip to actually taste one of my desserts, then he'll take me on for sure."

Dad smiles and gives my elbow a squeeze. "He'd be a fool not to," he says.

Thankfully, our food comes and my parents go back to having strained but polite conversation. I glance at Mr. Hammond, who looks totally uncomfortable. I don't blame him. Is this what my family is going to be like from now on?

Chapter 8

That night, as I'm flipping through a huge French recipe book that I got out of the library, trying to figure out what dessert will wow Chip Ackerson, my phone beeps to tell me that the results of my Truth Game questionnaire are in. I look at my scores. Five points for the "Dating" one along with the comment: "Whoa, snooping in the underwear drawer? Two bonus points!" I smile for a second before it dawns on me that some complete stranger knows about me rummaging through Briana's underwear. Creepy.

I look at the stats to see how my answers stack up with other people's, expecting them to be pretty average. I'm shocked when I see that my numbers are pretty much opposite from everyone else's. Having a boyfriend but never having been kissed makes me a total anomaly.

Ugh. Just when I think I've left my middle school self behind, something else makes me feel like an outcast.

I start pacing around the kitchen, feeling like I should bake something. That's what I always do when I get stressed. I should probably try one of the French pastries I was looking at, but for some reason all I feel like baking are chocolate-chip cookies. No way. I'm not going to waste time making something I've baked a million times before.

"Mom!" I call into the living room. "What do you want me to bake for you?"

"How about some lemon squares?" she calls back. It figures. They're her favorite.

I sigh and get to work. Maybe I can make a meringue to go on top or do something to make the lemon squares a little fancier. At least the act of baking will calm me down. But the weird thing is, it doesn't. Not even when the squares are in the oven. Not even when I pull them out, all warm and gooey, and the whole house smells like heaven.

"Mmm," Mom says, her nose practically pulling her into the kitchen. "Can I have a bite?"

I push the entire pan over to her. "They're all yours."

"So I have some great news," Mom says. "One of the women on the PTA told me that her brother-in-law's cousin, Bianca, might be doing sound for the Cooking Network special! So, if you want, I can give her a call and set up a lunch meeting for you and Bianca this week!"

I blink at her. "Huh?"

"Don't you see? If you talk to Bianca and make a good impression, maybe she'll get you some face time with Chip." She gets a thoughtful look on her face. "Now, the first thing we need to do—"

"Mom, do you really think me having lunch with a complete stranger is going to help anything? You know what I'm like with people I don't know." I'd probably insult the woman's dog by accident or something.

"You'll be fine!" Mom says. Then she frowns. "Except she apparently speaks only Italian."

I groan. "I know you're trying to help, but can you give me a chance to figure things out on my own for once?"

Her face falls. "It's just…I've watched your shyness hold you back so many times. I didn't want that to happen again with something you really cared about."

As much as I hate to admit it, she's right. Normally, I wouldn't have the guts to do anything about getting onto the show. "I know, but I won't let that happen. Can you please let me handle things my way?"

She puts her hand on mine. "I guess I'm still getting used to the idea that I don't have to look out for you all the time. It's like the day we got you that unicorn balloon at the fair when you were little. Do you remember? When it flew away, you were so upset that I rushed out and bought you a new one, even though I knew I should use that opportunity to teach you about taking better care of your possessions. I told myself I had plenty of time to teach you about the harsh facts of life when you were older. But I think part of me is still trying to protect you from them."

The funny thing is, I remember that day with the unicorn balloon, but in my memory, it was my dad who got me a new one when the first one blew away. He's always seemed like the parent who would bend over backward to make me smile. I guess I forget that my mom's always protected me too, just in a different way.

"If you need my help, I'm here. Okay?" she says.

"Thanks," I say. And even though I appreciate her letting me solve my own problems for once, I also sort of miss the days when my mom could buy me a new balloon and everything would be perfect again.

● ● ●

When I get to the bakery the next day, I'm shocked to see Briana actually doing some work until I realize it's because Cherie's in the room. The minute she's not around, it's guaranteed Briana will stop wrapping up muffins and go back to playing with her phone.

"Oh, Rachel, you're here," Cherie says. "Can I talk to you in my office for a second?"

My stomach flips. "Is everything okay?" I ask as I follow her.

She closes the door and motions for me to sit. "Well…I know you really want to work here, but right now I'm not sure your work ethic is as strong as I'd like to see it."

"My-my work ethic? Did I do something wrong?"

"I was looking back over the candy satchels that you and Briana were working on yesterday, and several of them really weren't up to par. When I asked Briana about it, she said she noticed you were having some trouble with them. If you needed help, I wish you'd asked."

My mouth sags open. "Briana said *I* was having trouble with them?" I can't believe this. Yesterday, I showed Briana how to tie the satchels three times, and each time she just shrugged and did it her way. I finally gave up and went through and fixed the ones she'd done after she was gone, but I must have missed a few. "No-no. *I* was fine. Briana was the one…" But I can tell Cherie doesn't want to listen to excuses, so I sigh and say, "I'll make sure we both do better."

"Excellent. Now get out there and give it your all, okay?"

Ugh. Apparently my all isn't good enough with Briana around.

I shoot Briana a dirty look as I get to work wrapping the muffins she abandoned. She, of course, doesn't lift a finger to help, and I don't ask. I rather do the whole list of daily tasks on my own and know it's done right than have Briana mess stuff up and then blame it on me again.

"Excuse me," I say a few minutes later, trying to push past her to get some Ryan's Bakery labels from under the counter. She stands there staring out the window, totally ignoring me. "Briana, I need to—"

Before I can finish, she suddenly dives behind the counter like she's stepped into an elevator shaft. An instant later, the bakery door opens, and Angela Bareli comes in.

"Hey, Rachel," Angela says, sounding downright friendly. "I didn't know you work here."

"Oh yeah," I say, trying to ignore the fact that Briana is crouched about two feet away from me. It's obvious she doesn't want Angela to see her, but I can't figure out why.

I'm tempted to out her—she definitely wouldn't hesitate to do it to me—but I'm not that mean-spirited...or that brave. "I started a few days ago."

"That's great! I bet you can help me. I want to get a cake for my birthday party, but I have no idea what I want. You're the perfect person to ask since you're amazing with that kind of stuff."

Wow. Angela was always my biggest competition during the Spring Dance baking competition in middle school. Of course, it turned out she totally cheated and got a bakery to make her entries for her, but I never expected her to actually compliment my baking skills, considering how much time she spent trying to outdo me.

"Sure," I say. "Do you have a theme for the party?"

"Not really. But it's going to be huge, like the kind we had in elementary school. Remember when we'd invite all the kids in our class? I don't want to leave anyone out, so I'm inviting everybody."

"The whole grade?" I say in disbelief.

She smiles. "Why not? It'll be fun! And maybe I could get a pony or something." She gasps. "Oh my gosh! That could be the theme! A little kid birthday party!"

I guess if our entire grade could fit in someone's house,

it would be Angela's. It's the biggest one in her neighborhood. But I doubt Marisol would appreciate having a raging party happening next door, especially with a pony tromping through the yard.

I write down how many people Angela is hoping to feed and when she would need the cake, and then I pick her brain about what flavors and textures she likes and doesn't like. I expect to get a rush of ideas like I normally do the minute I start thinking about desserts. When I heard the Montelle-Brennan wedding is going to be by the water, for example, I instantly pictured a cream-colored cake covered in seashells. But nothing happens this time.

"We'll take care of everything," I tell her.

"You're the best! Thank you!" she says, and then she hugs me over the counter. Angela Bareli, backstabbing social climber, *hugs me*. I nearly die from the shock. But then she pulls away and gives me a little smile before rushing off.

"She's gone," I say to Briana, who's managed to wedge herself under the counter so her head is almost inside a box of napkins.

She lets out a long breath and then gets to her feet, smoothing her apron. Then she goes back to tapping her phone as if nothing happened.

"Are you going to tell me what that was all about?" I finally say.

She snorts. "Like you'd want the biggest gossip at school seeing you at some stupid job," she says. "So embarrassing."

I don't bother pointing out that Angela did see me at my "stupid job" and that there was nothing embarrassing about it. "Angela seems really different this year. Maybe she doesn't gossip like she used to."

"Yeah, right. As if people ever really change. She's still the same old Angela."

"I'd like to think that I've changed," I say softly. Honestly, last year I wouldn't have been capable of having this conversation with Briana. I would have been way too intimidated around her to even open my mouth.

"Well, I haven't," Briana declares. "And I don't want to. What's so great about changing anyway?"

Before I can answer, my phone beeps in my pocket. It's a message from Marisol. I expect it to be about the Fashion Club or Andrew's movie, since that's pretty much all she can talk about these days, so I almost drop the phone when I see what she's written. **Are you sitting down? Guess who I saw at the grocery store?? Chet Ackerson!**

I stare at the message in shock, holding back a shriek.

Do you mean CHIP Ackerson???? I write back. It can't be true. What would Chip be doing in town so far ahead of the wedding special? But maybe he's one of those hosts who like to go to the place where they're shooting and get a feel for it before the show. For all I know, he's been wandering around town for days, and I didn't even realize it. We could have even been breathing the same air!

Yes! The Pastry Wars guy, Marisol writes back, and this time I can't stop myself from shrieking.

Chapter 9

"Tell me everything," I say, perching on Marisol's bed. "What was Chip doing? Did he say anything? Does he look the same in person as he does on TV?"

"Whoa!" Marisol says. "I only know who he is thanks to you. I was with my mom at the store, buying some cantaloupe, and there he was picking out a pineapple."

I suck in a breath. "Pineapple?" This has to be a sign from the gods.

"Yeah, he kept picking up different ones, sniffing them, and then putting them back."

"He was testing for ripeness," I say. "If they don't smell sweet, that means they were picked too early and don't have enough sugar to ripen."

"Thanks, Foodipedia," Marisol says with a laugh. "Anyway, I looked it up after I got home, and it turns out some of the Cooking Network people are already in town doing stuff for the wedding special. And"—she grins—"this is the best part. I called the hotels in the area until I found out where Chet's staying."

I don't bother correcting her this time. "No way! Where?"

She describes a little inn in the center of town that I've never really paid attention to. "So what are you going to do?" she asks.

"I just have to show him I can bake," I tell her. "I'll drop some pastries off at the inn for him tomorrow. He'll take one bite and know he made a huge mistake, right?"

"Totally," Marisol says.

I grab my cooking notebook out of my bag and start flipping through, but nothing seems right. I need something bigger, something fancier, something that will really wow Chip. I start looking up "super-fancy desserts" on my phone and find a couple things that are really impressive, but they're also covered in edible gold and stuff. No way can I afford to do that! Finally, I find some delicious-looking cream puff things that are dribbled with chocolate.

"How do you pronounce *religieuse*?" I ask Marisol. I'm definitely going to know how to pronounce the name of what I'm making this time.

Marisol keeps typing away for a minute before looking up. "Huh? Oh, sorry. Ms. Emerald wants me to fill out all this stuff about club goals and agendas. She said she doesn't have time to advise a new club unless she's sure I'm totally serious about it. By the time she'll actually let me start the Fashion Club, it'll be June already." She sighs. "Sorry. You have my undivided attention now."

I start to tell Marisol about the pastries I've been looking up, but after a minute, her eyes wander back to her laptop again. I give up when my phone beeps. It's another Truth Game questionnaire. This one is about jobs. Since Marisol is busy anyway, I start working on the questions.

1. Do you have an after-school job?

Since there's no "more than one" option, I simply say "yes."

2. Are you a good employee?

If you asked Cherie and Chef Ryan, I'm not sure what they'd say, but since I know I'm doing my best, I choose "yes" again.

3. Do you like your job?

That's a tricky one. Do I love cleaning houses with Mom? No, but it's not so bad. On the other hand, I thought I'd love working at the bakery, but so far it hasn't been nearly as great as I'd hoped. Still, I'm hoping it'll get better, so I finally settle on "I don't know."

4. What's something people would be surprised to find out about your job?

This one's easy. "That my grade's former queen bee works at a bakery with me! She wants people to think she's better than they are, but I saw her taking out the trash yesterday, and I swear some rotting fruit dripped on her shoe."

Briana only took the trash out, of course, because Chef Ryan asked her to and then watched her the whole time. Otherwise, I'm sure I would have gotten stuck with the task. She was scrunching her nose so hard the whole time that I thought it would retract into her face.

5. Dare time! Do something at work that you know you'd get in trouble for if someone

found out. Write about it here in the next
forty-eight hours for bonus points!

Yeah, right. As if I'm going to risk getting fired just to
get bonus points on some game.

"What are you working on?" Marisol asks, making me
jump. "You keep making weird sounds, like you're thinking really hard."

"It's this game Briana signed me up for," I say. Then I
try to explain it to Marisol. I can tell by the frown on her
face that she gets it even less than I did when Briana first
explained it to me. That's one reason I haven't told her
about it until now. I figured she wouldn't really be into it.

"Why would you answer those questions?" she says.
"Who knows what kind of evil stuff the company who
made that is going to use your answers for? Andrew was
telling me that if social media sites are free, that means
you're the product. The company makes money off selling
data about you."

"Actually," I say before she can go on a full-on tirade,
"it's not a company. It's some high school kid. And it's just
for fun."

Marisol still looks skeptical. "If Briana Riley plays it,

how much fun can it be? And what if people find out what you wrote?"

"Briana said it's totally anonymous. And she also said that—"

"Wait." Marisol holds her hands up. "Are you actually quoting Briana Riley? Since when do you agree with a word she says?"

"I-I don't," I stammer. "She was explaining how it works, that's all. Anyway, the game's actually pretty fun."

"If you say so," Marisol says, and for some reason I can't help feeling annoyed. Just because it's not her thing, does that mean I shouldn't play the Truth Game either?

"Oh!" Marisol says, jumping to her feet. "I forgot to show you!" She hurries to her closet and pulls out a bright-orange dress. "What do you think? It's not done yet, but this is what I'm making for Ms. Emerald."

"It's pretty," I say, even though I actually think it's kind of hideous. Marisol and I don't always have the same taste in clothes, but she always manages to make things look good. Hopefully once it's done, I'll understand her "creative vision" a little better.

She asks me about my opinion on the beading she's going to put around the collar, but I'm too distracted by how awkward things suddenly feel between us to give her much of an answer. Who would have thought the day would come when I'd have an easier time talking to my worst enemy than to my best friend?

Chapter 10

"Wake up, sleepyhead," Mom says as we get in the car to head to our first cleaning job of the day. I barely slept last night because I was so busy stressing about the chocolate-raspberry macaroons I wound up making for Chip Ackerson. They're good, and way fancier than the stuff I normally make, but I don't know if they're special enough. I mean, he eats unbelievable pastries all the time. Mine have to stand out.

Then, when I did finally manage to fall asleep, I dreamed about kissing a giant octopus that had Evan's face. Its slimy tentacles kept getting in the way so that our lips never even touched. Blech!

We pull up to the Town Center Inn, and I take a deep breath before heading out of the car, my plate of plastic-wrap-covered pastries clutched to my chest. I'd been hoping to wear my lucky shirt today, the one I stained with toothpaste on the first day of school, but I couldn't find it anywhere. Hopefully that's not a bad omen.

As I walk, I mumble what I'm going to say under my breath. "Hi! I'm Rachel Lee. I auditioned for *Pastry Wars* and didn't get in, but I think if you try these pastries, you'll see that I deserve another chance."

When I go in, I'm surprised to see the inn is tiny and decorated with old quilts and tacky wooden vases. Not exactly the kind of place where I'd expect a big-time TV personality to be staying, but maybe he's trying to fly under the radar. Or maybe there aren't a lot of good housing options in town. The hotel where Dad is staying is basically a row of beige boxes.

When I get to the front desk, a man with a looping gray mustache beams back at me. "How can I help you?" he asks.

"I'm looking for one of your guests. Mr. Ackerson?" I whisper, in case him staying here is a secret.

The man looks up the name. "I'm afraid he's not here right now. I can leave a message for him."

"Oh." Of course he's not here. He's probably off doing location scouting or something. "Can I leave something in his room?"

"Sorry!" the man says cheerfully. "Can't do that. But if you'd like to leave it with me, I'll be sure he gets it."

I glance down at the plate. I worked so hard on these. Can I really hand them over to anyone but Chip? But what choice do I have? If I didn't have to work at the bakery today, I'd camp out in front of the inn all day, but that's not an option.

"Okay…" I say, handing the plate over.

"Ooh, these look delicious," the man says, the ends of his mustache twitching. "I'll be sure Mr. Ackerson gets them."

That'll have to be good enough. I thank him and rush back to my mom's car.

"Well, did you meet him?" she practically shrieks.

I shake my head and tell her what happened. As we pull away, Mom looks almost as disappointed as I feel.

* * *

In between afternoon cleaning jobs, my phone beeps, telling me that I have yet another new Truth Game questionnaire waiting for me. This one is called "Friends." Since Mom is deep in thought as we drive across town, I decide to take a look.

1. Do you have a best friend?

That's easy. Marisol has been my best (and, until recently, only) friend for years. Definitely "yes."

2. Have you ever told your best friend a major lie?

Ugh. The truth is, I've lied to Marisol more times than I'd like to count. When your best friend's moral compass is pretty much stuck at north all the time, sometimes it's easier to hide stuff from her than admit to totally messing up. But I've sworn to Marisol that I'll be honest with her from now on, so I don't feel totally terrible when I answer "yes."

3. Do you ever wish you were best friends with someone else?

I start to choose "no," but my fingers hesitate without my brain's approval. I love Marisol, of course. She's the only person in the world who'd go along with my crazy schemes and forgive me for being a total idiot sometimes. But I can't help thinking about how things have felt off between us lately, especially last night. We used to be so in sync, but now…I don't want a different best friend, not exactly. I wish that she was still a little more like the old Marisol, that's all. Finally, I choose "I don't know."

4. What's something about your best friend that would surprise people if they knew?

I think for a second and then write, "That she's not as honest as she thinks she is. She's always going on about being up-front with everyone, but she's been lying to her mom about dating A. Her mom would freak out if she knew, and I bet A would freak out if he knew their relationship was a secret."

5. Dare time! Do something to show your best friend how you feel about him or her. Write about it here in the next forty-eight hours for bonus points!

That one's easy. Maybe I can make Marisol some cookies or something and show her that even if we're both super busy with our own lives right now, she's still my BFF. Or maybe I'll make pineapple upside-down cake and hopefully it'll jog her memory about the pine-apple gods.

We pull up to Caitlin Schubert's house, and I quickly close the app and put my phone away. Inside, Caitlin's mom, Ms. Montelle, is bustling around the house like she can't figure out where she left her head.

"Thank goodness you're here!" she says. "This house is such a mess that I can't even find my to-do lists for the wedding." She laughs. "First thing on the list? Clean the house."

Mom smiles and assures her that we'll take care of everything. Over the summer, we were afraid we'd lost Ms. Montelle as a client, but now that Mom is working with Ladybug Cleaners, we're back to doing her house every weekend. I don't even dread seeing Caitlin, though I doubt the two of us will ever be best friends or anything.

"Who said planning a wedding in a month was a good idea?" Ms. Montelle is saying as she paces around the kitchen. "I must have been out of my mind!"

Mom gives a sympathetic chuckle. "You'll be great. Everything will work out."

"Caitlin's been so helpful, but knowing we're going to be on TV puts that much more pressure on everything!"

"You can rest assured that the catering will be perfect. Rachel here works at Ryan's Bakery now."

Ms. Montelle turns to me. "You do? That's wonderful!"

I shrug. "I won't be there the day of the wedding though. I'll be back at the bakery. But Bri—" I freeze, remembering I'm not supposed to tell anyone about Briana being there. How is she going to keep Caitlin (or anyone) from seeing her at the wedding when Cherie will probably have her running around all day setting stuff up? But I definitely don't want to be the one to spill Briana's secret, so I keep my mouth shut.

"Hi there!" a friendly looking man with a graying beard calls from the hallway. "I'm Paul Brennan! The fiancé!" He comes over and enthusiastically shakes our hands, like he's thrilled to meet us. He seems just as nice as Ms. Montelle and not at all what I expected a rich, big-shot guy to be like.

Ms. Montelle smiles and puts her arm around his waist. "This whole thing has gotten so big so fast! We wanted a nice, small wedding. But as long as the groom shows up, I'll be happy."

"Hmm," he says, pretending to mull that over. "I'll see if I can fit it into my calendar."

"And a delicious wedding cake wouldn't hurt either." She gives me a little wink.

As I watch Ms. Montelle and Mr. Brennan drive off to an appointment with the florist, I suddenly have an image of their perfect wedding cake again. It's still covered in seashells, but this time, it's a soft-blue color with a few pops of yellow to reflect their sunny personalities.

I shake the image out of my head. Not only will I never be allowed to touch their wedding cake, but I know the one Chef Ryan is planning is way more intricate than the one in my head. There's no way they'd be into something so ordinary.

When Mom and I are almost done cleaning, Caitlin comes through the door with Steve Mueller. I freeze. Oh my goldfish. Steve Mueller is going to see me covered in grime and sweat and sporting neon cleaning gloves! But then I remember: I don't care about Steve Mueller anymore. Not only is he dating Caitlin now, but I have a much better guy in my life who actually knows I exist. Still, I tear off my gloves and smooth back my hair, trying to look as presentable as possible. Just because my crush on Steve is gone doesn't mean I want him to see me looking like a house elf.

"Oh hey, Rachel," Caitlin says, and it almost sounds friendly coming out of her mouth. "How's it going?"

"Good." I swallow, forcing myself to talk to her like we're not on totally different ends of the popularity chain. "That's so crazy that you won the Cooking Network contest!"

Her face lights up. "I know, right? I never thought I'd have a chance. My mom thinks it's pretty cool, but I don't think she understands how amazing it is. You're a big fan too, aren't you?"

"That's kind of an understatement," I say with a laugh.

Steve lets out a good-natured groan. "I don't get why people watch shows about food. I'd rather just eat it."

Caitlin gives him a playful jab in the side. How come when *she* does it, she doesn't end up hitting her boyfriend's funny bone? "If I didn't watch all those shows, I wouldn't know how to make you all those cookies you like."

He grins. "Good point."

"I should get back to work," I mumble.

But as I start to drag the vacuum away, Caitlin stops me. "By the way, have you seen Briana lately? I've been trying to call her, but she's been kind of MIA."

The question totally catches me off guard. Since when is Briana's best friend asking me about her? Wait. Does she know that Briana and I work together?

I must look confused because she adds, "I figured since

you and Evan are a thing, maybe you go over to their house sometimes."

Ah. I guess the job is a secret after all. "I don't know. I think she's been pretty busy."

Caitlin sighs. "I feel like she's been avoiding me lately. Is she okay?"

"I think so," I say, but then I remember how worried Evan's been about her and how sad she looked at the bakery the other day. How can I tell Caitlin about that without giving away Briana's secret?

Steve waves his hand dismissively. "She's fine. It's Briana. That girl can bounce back from anything. Remember when she got hit in the head during a softball game last year, and instead of going to the hospital, she went to get her hair done?"

Caitlin lets out a soft laugh. I realize it might be the first time I've ever heard her laugh. I guess Steve must have that effect on her. "She did wind up with really hideous highlights, but otherwise she was fine."

"Rachel!" Mom calls from down the hall. "Are you ready to go?"

"Coming!" I say. Then I give them an awkward wave and head down the hall with my vacuum.

Chapter 11

Dad's not at Molly's when I get there for Sunday brunch, so I sit by the entrance and start working on another Truth Game questionnaire. I'm starting to see why Briana is so into this game. For her, it's all about proving how much better she is than all the other kids at our school. For me, it's about seeing how much I have in common with them.

I've always felt like a total outsider, but maybe I'm not as different from everyone as I thought. The numbers say so. Sixty percent of the people who answered the jobs questionnaire had the same answers as me. Sixty! That makes me in the majority! I'm willing to bet that's the first time that's ever happened.

This questionnaire is all about parents.

1. Do you get along with your parents?

Mom and I used to be on totally different planets, but now we actually get along really well, even if she does still drive me a little nutty sometimes. And my dad might be a big kid sometimes, but he always listens. I choose "yes."

2. Do they understand you?

This is a tough one. Mom tries to understand me, but we're so different that I think sometimes we can't figure each other out. And now that Dad and I have been apart for a while, I feel like we're not always on the same page anymore. I finally pick "I don't know."

3. Do you ever wish you were born to someone else?

I think about that for a minute and realize that I can honestly say "no." Mom and I might not have always gotten along, but she's always been a total rock in my life, even when I didn't deserve it. When I think about all the stuff I've done—lying to her, stealing money from my bank account, etc.—it's a miracle she's still speaking to me! Compared to Evan's mom, who doesn't seem to support him unless he's doing what she wants him to do, I realize how lucky I am to have mine. In fact, I'll have to remember to give her a big hug when I get home. My response is "No!"

4. What's one thing no one knows about your parents?

5. For bonus points, we dare you to show your parents how you feel about them in the next twenty-four hours and tell us about it here!

I don't get to write anything for the last two questions because Dad rushes through the door. "Sorry I'm late, Roo!" he says.

I can't help noticing how grimy he looks. And for some reason, he's wearing an orange life jacket. "What did you do, jump ship?" I ask, quoting *Back to the Future*, one of his favorite movies.

"Oops! I forgot I had this on." He grins as he pulls off the life vest. "Guess what? I got a new job!"

"You're not doing boat tours again, are you?" In Florida,

Dad did scuba and snorkeling trips along the coast, but considering it's almost fall and we're in New England, I doubt that's going to work very well this time.

"Nope!" he says. "I'm the new manager of a canoe and kayak shop."

I stare at him for a second. "Do you know anything about canoes and kayaks?" I can't help asking, getting serious déjà vu to last year when my dad took one scuba class and decided he was meant to go teach classes in a whole other part of the country. Did he catch one glimpse of a kayak and realize it was his new life's calling?

"Actually," he says, "I used to go kayaking with your grandpa all the time when I was a kid."

"Really? I don't think you've ever told me about that."

He chuckles. "I'd forgotten, to be honest. It was so long ago. But we'd go almost every weekend when I was growing up. I loved being out on the water. Maybe that's why the idea of starting a scuba business spoke to me."

"But isn't it getting too cold for that kind of thing?" I ask.

"Business *is* slow during the winter," he admits, "but the shop recently moved to a bigger location, and they're looking to expand. They want to branch out into selling skiing and indoor rock-climbing equipment, and to help them."

"But you've never even been rock climbi

Dad grins. "There's only one way to fix that. I'm taking a rock-climbing class this weekend. Do you want to take it with me?"

"Um, Dad? Have you seen me try to walk up and down stairs? That's dangerous enough."

"I'm serious, Roo. It'll be fun. And who knows, maybe this will be the thing we do together on weekends now that I'm back in town, just like my dad and I used to go kayaking."

When he puts it like that, I can't say no. Besides, the questionnaire about my parents is still bouncing around in my head. If I go risk my life for my dad, that's certainly showing him how much I care about him, right?

After we order our usual crepes, Dad asks me all about school and my job. I can't get over how weird and yet normal it is to have him around to talk to about all these things. I didn't realize how much I missed it.

"I'm so glad you came back," I tell him.

"I know, Roo. Me too."

"And just in time for my big TV debut!" I say. Then I tell him about dropping the macaroons off for Chip Ackerson

.s morning. "I wish I could have seen the look on his face when he tasted them, but I'll have to imagine it."

"What did you say in your note?" Dad asks.

"Note?"

"When you left the cookies for him, you left a note, right? So he'd know who they were from."

I stare at him, horror creeping through my entire body. "Oh my goldfish," I whisper. "I didn't leave a note." How could I be so stupid? "I practiced what I was going to say to him, but when he wasn't there, I guess I kind of got flustered and…" I bury my face in my hands. "I can't believe it. Even if he loved them, it doesn't matter because he had no clue who they were from!"

"It's okay, Roo."

"It's not okay! I keep messing things up." At this rate, I'll never get another shot at being on the show.

"Just try again tomorrow," Dad says.

He's right. Tomorrow I'll go back over with a new batch of pastries, signed this time. But what if it's not enough? Once the Montelle-Brennan wedding is over, Chip Ackerson will be gone again. If I'm really going to make this happen, I need to do whatever it takes to convince Chip to give me another chance.

Chapter 12

U m, excuse me," I squeak at the couple in full lip-lock in front of my locker. Of course, they don't hear me. "Um, that's my locker," I try again.

They pull apart long enough to give me a dirty look before they move over about three inches and resume their make-out session. Gross.

As I inch open my locker door, I spot another smooching couple at the end of the hall. Is this what people are supposed to do when they're in high school?

I carefully close my locker again and head off to gym class, excited to see Evan even if it's only from the other side of the room.

The whole time we're playing dodgeball—me with the girls and Evan with the boys—I can't stop thinking about the Truth Game results. How can I be the only one in the whole school, probably in the whole town, who has a boyfriend but has never had a real kiss? Do other people kiss right away like it's not a big deal? Is this yet another thing that I was supposed to know and totally missed somehow?

As I pause to adjust my too-tight sports bra, I hear Angela Bareli suddenly yell "Rachel, look out!" a second before something hard and rubbery smacks me right behind my ear.

"Oof!" I say, staggering sideways as the ball bounces away from me and rolls into the corner.

"Lee, are you okay?" Mrs. Da Silva yells. Then she blows her whistle and does a slow jog over to me.

My ear is ringing, and my head feels like it's not on quite right, but otherwise I think I'm okay. When I tell her that, she asks me to follow her pencil (the one she always keeps tucked behind her ear) with my eyes while she waves it in front of my nose. I guess I must pass the test because she simply says, "You need to pay more attention to your surroundings, Lee," and tells me to go sit on the bleachers for the last few minutes of class.

Evan flashes me an "Are you okay?" look across the gym. I give him a weak thumbs-up and sink onto a bench, wiping the sweat from my forehead. Why do the other girls in my class all glow with perspiration, and I have rivers of sweat trickling down my forehead the minute I even think about doing any physical activity?

For the next couple minutes, my head still ringing like a glass jar, I watch Evan play. I can't get over how coordinated he is. The ball doesn't come close to smacking him in the head, not even once.

Finally, Mrs. Da Silva tells us to go get changed. Instead of heading to the locker room though, Evan heads straight toward me.

"Are you sure you're okay?" he says. "I heard that ball hit you from the other side of the gym."

"I'm great," I tell him. Knowing he's so concerned about me makes me feel a whole lot better, in fact. For some reason, I can't help staring at his lips and trying to figure out if they look kissable. Would they be dry or wet or soft or sticky?

"Rachel?" he asks.

But why am I thinking about all of this? I'm not exactly going to kiss him right this second. Or am I? The Truth Game dared me to do it. Maybe the game was right.

Weird energy starts buzzing through my whole body like someone plugged me into an electrical outlet. Normally I'd sit around and wait for something to happen, hoping the right moment will come along. But maybe it's finally time to stop thinking about kissing the guy and actually *do it*.

So I do. I grab Evan's shirt and pull him toward me.

"Wha—?" he starts to say, but then my lips are mashed up against his and he can't say anything.

As our lips meet, I expect to feel butterflies and to hear angels and to see fireworks. Instead, all I feel is sweat, *my* sweat dribbling down my temple. And all I hear is Evan's breathing, quick and panicked-sounding, almost like he's drowning. And all I see—wait. Why are my eyes open? My eyes shouldn't be open! And his are open too. They're so wide and so close to my face that it's actually kind of scary.

I stagger back, pulling my lips away. Evan blinks at me, looking like *he* was the one smacked in the head with a dodgeball.

"Are-are you okay?" I stammer, wiping the sweat from my upper lip. I can't help noticing how very wet Evan's lips look too. Oh my goldfish. Did my sweat drip on him while we were kissing?

"Lee! Riley!" Mrs. Da Silva yells across the gym. "No canoodling in my class!"

A few of the kids nearby snicker as they head to the

locker rooms. Holy baked rhubarb. Did that just happen? Did I actually kiss Evan Riley during gym class?

"Where did that come from?" Evan says finally.

"I-I'm sorry," I stammer because I don't know what else to say.

"Don't be sorry," he says. "I was just surprised." He reaches out and takes my hand in his. "Really, I didn't mind at all."

"Lee! Riley! To the locker rooms or to the principal's office, you decide."

We have no choice but to let go of each other's hands and rush away, but Evan flashes me a little smile over his shoulder. I did it. I can't believe I did it! I kissed Evan Riley! Suddenly, it feels like I've earned all the bonus points in the world.

Chapter 13

During the first hour of my shift at the bakery that afternoon, I keep hearing Chef Ryan grunting and cursing in the back as he works on a wedding cake. Briana barely even blinks as she stares at her phone, while I try to ignore the sounds as I pack up cupcakes and help customers.

The phone rings, and Briana stares at it like she's never seen a phone before.

I sigh and grab it even though talking on the phone is *so* not my forte. "Ryan's Bakery."

"Rachel? It's Angela. Is Chef Ryan nearby?"

"No, he's in the back room—"

Crash!

"Oh good. It was you I wanted to talk to. He showed me a sketch of the cake he's thinking about for my birthday party, and it's kind of boring. I mean it's pretty and stuff, but it doesn't really scream little kid party, you know?"

"Did you try telling him that?"

"He said it would look better in person, but I'm starting to get worried. Any chance you could talk to him for me?"

I gulp. "I can try. He's not the easiest person to talk to."

"I would super appreciate it! Everything else for my party is going to be so perfect. The cake has to be too, you know?"

I do know, so I promise her I'll take care of it, and then I hang up the phone. Another loud crash rings out in the kitchen, and I hear Chef Ryan let out a lionlike roar of frustration. I steel myself and tell Briana to watch the store for a minute. Then I peek my head into the kitchen, ready to retreat if need be.

Chef Ryan is hunched over a four-tiered cake, a bag of icing shaking in his hands. I take a step forward and almost wipe out on a glob of frosting on the floor. That's when I notice the frosting clinging to the walls and dripping from the countertops. What the Shrek?

"Is everything all right?" I ask.

Chef Ryan's eyes shoot up at me. "Fine." Then he scrunches his face up in concentration and goes back to shakily holding the icing bag over the top of the cake. "Who ever heard of a bee-themed wedding?" he grumbles.

"Bees?" I say with a shudder. As I inch closer, I see that Chef Ryan is covering the cake with tiny little flowers. Except they're lopsided. And they have wings. "Wait, they're having you draw bees on their cake?"

Chef Ryan sighs in frustration and takes a step back. "Hundreds of them. I've been working on them for hours, but my hands are so cramped up that I can't do any more. And the cake needs to be done tonight."

"Maybe I could help," I say softly.

He gives me a long look, and I expect him to shoot me down. So I almost die of shock when he nods in defeat and says, "Fine." He wipes his free hand on his apron. "But I'll be watching the whole time. Got it?"

I nod. This is it. My big chance to show him what I can do!

He ceremonially hands over the icing bag like it's a crown. I carefully get in position and realize my hands are shaking with nerves. If I do this right, hundreds of people will see this cake. They'll probably even take pictures of it and post them online! And if I mess it up... Well, it's better not to think about that.

I gulp in a breath and get to work. Slowly, I make one tiny bee, as similar to the ones on the bottom tier as I can. It looks like an ant.

Chef Ryan sighs. "Maybe I should—"

"No, let me try to fix it!" I say. Then I carefully fill in the wings and round out the body. When I'm finished, I'm relieved to see that it looks more bee than ant. I glance at Chef Ryan, and he only nods. That's all the encouragement I'm going to get, but it's enough.

I make another bee. And another. After the third one, I realize I'm barely breathing. No wonder my entire chest hurts.

Finally, I get into a rhythm where I'm icing and breathing at the same time. And I have to say, the bees look pretty good! The wings aren't quite as perfect as Chef Ryan's, but they look like little insects. When I get to the last one, I even manage to give it a little smile.

I step back, realizing that for a minute I actually forgot Chef Ryan was looming over me. When I glance at him, he's looking back at me with an expression that's totally unreadable. I guess this is what people mean when they say someone has a poker face.

"Well?" I say. "Is it okay?"

He gives it one more look, like he's searching for flaws, and then he nods. "It's okay," he says. "Now get back out front."

"W-wait," I say. "I was wondering about your plan for Angela Bareli's cake, the little kid birthday one?"

He sighs. "It'll be fine. Don't worry about it."

"But maybe I could—"

"Rachel," he says, his voice softening a little. "I appreciate your enthusiasm, but you have to crawl—"

"Before you can walk," I finish. "I know, I know."

"Now get back to work," he says, and the conversation is over.

Chapter 14

Whenever I go over to Evan's house, I dread Briana opening the door. This time when I ring the bell after dinner, it's even worse. His mom is the one whose unsmiling face greets me in the doorway.

"Oh hello, Rachel," she says. "Come in. Evan is in the family room." Her stiff tone makes it sound like she still sees me as the cleaning lady's daughter and not like her son's girlfriend, even though Mom and I haven't cleaned the Rileys' house in weeks. "How is your mother?"

"She's good," I say. "Um, busy."

Mrs. Riley sighs. "I may have to give her a call again. Our latest housekeeper has been far from stellar."

I bite back a smile. If Mrs. Riley tried to hire Ladybug Cleaners, I have no doubt Mom would say no. After Mom found me trying to vacuum up pieces of glass that Briana had oh-so-nicely sprinkled all over her bedroom carpet, she made it pretty clear that we were done putting up with the Riley drama. Thank goodness Evan is nothing like the rest of his family!

I find him in the family room among mountains of files. "What is all this?" I ask.

Evan sighs. "My dad asked me to help him clean out his home office. I'm supposed to sort all these files and put them in alphabetical order. It's taking forever."

"Need some help?" I ask.

He gives me a grateful smile. "I asked my sister, but she laughed in my face."

"Were you really surprised?" I can't help asking.

"I know, but I keep thinking the twin thing will kick in sometime." Upstairs, a door slams, and Evan gives me a crooked grin. No doubt that's Briana storming around up there.

As I sit down next to him on the carpet, I realize this is the closest I've been to him since our gym class kiss. I'm suddenly really aware of how much (or little) space is between us. Should I sit closer to him? Is that what couples who've kissed do?

I think about those couples I saw making out in the hallway. I don't want to be obnoxious like they were, but I also don't want to be afraid of holding hands with my own boyfriend! Now that I've been brave enough to kiss him, I can't start wimping out again.

I inch toward him on the couch until our knees are less than six inches apart.

"How's stuff going at the bakery?" he asks, leafing through a file folder. He doesn't seem to notice that I've moved closer, so I scoot over a little more. Five inches apart. Four. I can practically feel the heat from his knee radiating into mine.

"Okay," I say, and tell him about Chef Ryan finally letting me help out with one of the cakes this afternoon and about Angela's cake.

By the time I'm finished telling him about work, I'm so close to him that our legs are actually resting against each other. Evan doesn't move his away, so he either doesn't notice or doesn't mind. I can't believe I was so freaked out about the idea of kissing Evan at the airport before I went to visit my dad, and now I'm the one making the first move!

"So I was thinking," I say slowly, "that I should make my own cake for Angela's party."

Evan's eyebrows go up. "How will Chef Ryan feel about that?"

"I don't know," I admit. "But if I do an awesome job, maybe he'll see that I deserve to do more at the bakery, and maybe he'll actually let me help with the Montelle-Brennan wedding cake." Even if I can't get on TV, at least something I touched might.

"So what would you make?" he asks.

I sigh. "That's the problem. I've been totally uninspired recently. Everything I've come up with seems so boring. Want to help me think of some ideas?" I figure since he actually went to birthday parties when he was little—unlike super-shy me—he might have some pointers.

"Sure!" he says. "Well, I loved parties when I was a kid because it was the only time I was allowed to eat candy. And the cake was always this huge sheet cake with the kind of frosting that you could pull off in one swipe, you know?"

"Okay, what else?" I ask, taking out my baking journal. As he talks, I start furiously scribbling down notes.

"Although," he says finally, "if Angela's having a pony, then maybe you should go with the whole horse theme. Decorate the cake to look like a stable or something."

"Complete with manure?" I ask.

Evan laughs. Soon we're coming up with weirder and weirder cakes as we sort through his dad's files. My favorite is Evan's suggestion to make a perfectly innocent-looking cake that oozes green slime when you slice it. Angela would never forgive me for cake-sliming her, but imagining the look on her face is pretty hilarious.

"Maybe when I make another batch of pastries for Chip Ackerson, I should fill them with slime too," I say.

"That will definitely get his attention!" Evan says.

We're giggling so hard that I don't even realize I'm leaning against Evan, my head practically on his shoulder, until Briana stomps down the stairs and Evan jumps away from me on the couch. He has a weird, guilty look on his face, as if his sister caught us doing something wrong.

I expect Briana to glare at us or to ignore us and keep going, but instead she pauses in the doorway and says, "What are you two laughing about? I can hear you all the way upstairs."

Evan and I look at each other. I don't think either of us knows how to explain all the silly things we've been giggling over. "Slime," Evan says, and we start laughing again. But I can't help replaying that moment when he leaped away from me as if he was embarrassed to be seen so close to me, as if he couldn't get away from me fast enough.

Before Briana can say anything snide, Evan's dad comes

into the room. I've met him only a couple of times before, but I barely recognize him. His usually clean-shaven face is scruffy and haggard-looking, and his clothes are crumpled like he slept in them.

"Oh, hey," he says vaguely. "I was just…" He looks around like he forgot why he came into the room. "Water," he mumbles before wandering into the kitchen.

The three of us are silent for a minute after he's gone. "Um, is your dad okay?" I finally whisper.

"He's fine!" Briana says. "God, why do you have to be such a nosy freak?" Then she turns and runs back up the stairs.

Evan flashes me a sympathetic smile. "Sorry about her—" he starts to say, but I wave his apology away.

"Don't worry about it. I'm starting to learn not to take anything she says to heart." I clear my throat. "So, is your dad okay? I don't mean to be nosy, but he seems…"

"He's been kind of a mess since he lost his job," Evan says softly. "The whole thing blindsided him. One minute he was totally happy there, and then the next, they fired him because of some big misunderstanding."

"Wow," I say. "But you guys will be okay, right?" After my parents split up, my mom was constantly worried about paying the mortgage and stuff. Evan's house is so big and fancy that I can't imagine how much it must cost to live there.

"Dad has a couple interviews next week," Evan says, "so we're keeping our fingers crossed." He chuckles. "Especially my mom. It's driving her crazy to have him around so much."

"I'm sorry," I manage, not sure what else to say.

"Hey, it's not so bad. At least we get to be at the same school now, right?"

"Are you sure it's worth it?" I ask. "You loved your old school."

He smiles and squeezes my hand. "Yeah, but you weren't there. So how good could it really be?"

Holy freeze-dried cranberries. He is so cute. The doubts I had start to melt away. Whatever made him jump away from me, it had nothing to do with how he feels about me. Evan likes me and I like him. Plain and simple like vanilla ice cream.

Chapter 15

When I get home from Evan's, Mom is sitting on the couch absently flipping through TV channels. She's not even really looking at the screen, as if she's focused on something far away.

"Mom? Are you okay?"

She seems to snap back to reality. "Oh, Rachel! You're home!" She clears her throat. "Have a seat for a second, will you?"

Uh-oh. This can't be good.

"What's wrong?"

"Nothing is wrong! In fact, things are great!" She lets out a little chipmunk laugh that tells me things are *not* great.

I sit down and wait for her to spill. Luckily, it doesn't take long.

"Okay, you're going to think I'm nuts." She laughs again, even shriller this time. "Honestly, I think I must be nuts to even consider this! But Robert brought up the idea of us coming to live with him."

"Mr. Hammond?" I gasp. "Is this your weird way of telling me that you guys are getting married?" They've been together for only a few months, but I know they've already said the *L*-word. Still, that doesn't mean I'm ready to start thinking of him as my stepfather or anything. I mean, he keeps telling me to call him Robert, and I still can't stop referring to him as Mr. Hammond!

"No, nothing like that," Mom assures me. "Neither one of us is rushing to get into another marriage. But he lives in that big house all by himself, and we really care about each other. It wouldn't happen right away, of course. Maybe not at all. But I told him I'd think about it, and that I'd talk it over with you, of course."

I stare at her. My parents know how bad I am with change, so why do they keep throwing it at me every two seconds?

"Robert said you might not take this well," my mom adds.

I blink at her. "Why? What did he think I'd do?"

"Well," Mom says slowly, "you did take things a bit hard when you found out we were dating. Remember when you told him your father was only away on business, even though we all knew that wasn't true? And then there was all that nonsense about his underwear…"

I cringe, remembering the rumor I accidentally started about Mr. Hammond wearing adult diapers. "I didn't do that on purpose!"

"True. But you can't blame Robert for wondering if it was your way of lashing out at him because you were feeling threatened."

I stare at her. "But that's crazy!"

"I know you wouldn't do that," Mom says. "But look at it from his perspective. He's done nothing but try to get you to like him. Things are better now, but they started off a bit rough, didn't they? I think he's still not sure where you two stand."

"He's fine," I say. "We're fine. I like him and everything. I'm glad you're happy. But moving in with him… It feels like a lot, you know?"

Mom's face falls. "It was just a thought, but it's nothing that we need to consider right now. Forget I said anything, okay?"

I'm about to nod and pretend the whole conversation never happened. But then I think back to writing all that stuff about my mom in the Truth Game and how she's put up with so much of my drama recently. She's always trying to support me, even if she doesn't always go about it the right way. Maybe it's time I support her.

"Um, actually," I say slowly, "I think it's a great idea."

Mom's eyes widen. "You do?"

"You're right about Mr. Hammond's house. There's tons of room for all three of us."

"Really?" Mom practically squeals. "I'm so glad you're okay with the idea. I'll talk to Robert about a time frame and let you know, okay?" She reaches out and gives my arm a squeeze. "You really are growing up."

And even though the whole idea of packing up our house and moving in with my former vice principal is making my armpits slick with sweat, I can't help smiling back at her.

Chapter 16

This time when I go into the Town Center Inn, I feel prepared. Not only did I practice what I was going to say to Chip, but I also have a note attached to my plate of pastries. I went ahead and made the *religieuse* (after I looked up how to pronounce it) which is basically a cream puff with some chocolate layered in. It came out perfect.

I see the same guy with the twirled mustache at the front desk, and I start to wonder if anyone else works here.

"Hello there!" he says. "How can I help you?"

"Hi, I, um, dropped off some macaroons for Mr. Ackerson the other day, but I'm not sure he got them. And if he did, I don't know if he knew they were from me, so I brought something else for him. Um, so is he here?"

"Sorry! I can leave a message for him."

"Do you know if he liked the pastries I brought last time?"

The man gives me a blank look. "I'm sorry. I don't remember."

That makes me twice as nervous to leave the pastries. What if the man ate them? Or what if he forgot about them and never even gave them to Chip?

"Can't you tell me which room he's in so I can leave them outside his door?"

"No can do!" he says. "I'm happy to take them though."

Is it my imagination, or does he sound a little too eager to take them off my hands? "Never mind, I'll come back later," I say.

The man looks a tiny bit disappointed. "Okay."

I head toward the door, my heart pounding. I can't strike out again, but if I leave the pastries with this guy, there's no telling if Chip will actually get them. I lurk in the lobby for a minute, trying to decide what to do. Somehow Marisol roped me into being a production assistant for Andrew's documentary on school lunches, so I'm supposed to be at the school right now, but I feel like I can't leave here unless I've done something to reach out to Chip.

Then the phone at the front desk rings, and the man answers it. He listens for a minute, his face growing serious, and then he says, "I'll be right there with a fresh towel!"

He rushes over to a small office I hadn't noticed before and asks someone to watch the front desk for a second before he disappears down the hall. A woman who looks like she's definitely someone's grandmother goes over to stand behind the front desk. Maybe I'll have better luck with her.

"Hi, dear," she says when I go over. "How can I help you?"

"I really need your help," I say, trying a different approach this time. "I baked these pastries as a thank-you to one of your guests. He's not here right now, but I really want to leave them in front of his door so he'll be sure to get them."

"We can keep them up here at the desk for him," she says.

"I know, but I'd feel a lot better if they were delivered right to his room," I say. "I'm afraid someone will eat them or something."

She laughs. "My son does have a soft spot for sweets," she says. "If you leave them lying around, there's a chance he won't be able to help himself."

I knew it! The guy with the mustache must be her son, and he gobbled up my macaroons! "Please, can you put the pastries in his room for him? It's really, really important that he gets them. Please?"

I must sound as desperate as I feel because the woman finally nods and asks me for the last name. "Oh, he's one of the convention guests," she says as she looks up Chip's room number. I don't know what she's talking about, but all I care about is that my plan is actually working. "Okay, come with me."

I expect her to lead us to some kind of huge suite away from the other rooms, but Room 22 is about halfway down a hallway of rooms that seem like they're all the same. Chip must really be trying to fly under the radar so that people don't try to stalk him.

The woman knocks on the door, and when there's no answer, she unlocks it and takes the pastries from me. "Did you leave a note so he knows who they're from?"

"I did!" I say. I agonized over what to write for hours, but I finally settled on: "I hope these pastries give you a taste of what I'd bring to your show. Please give me another chance!" Then I'd left my name and contact info.

I watch the woman leave the plate on the nightstand and then I try to get a peek into the rest of the room, but she quickly closes the door again. "There," she says. "He's guaranteed to get them."

"Thank you!" I say, tempted to hug her. Instead, I hurry

down the hallway and get to the lobby just as the man at the front desk resumes his spot.

"Can I help you?" he asks, as if he's never met me before.

"Nope! I was just leaving!" I chirp. Then I hurry out the door, my body pulsing with excitement. *I did it!* Now all I have to do is wait.

● ● ●

"You kissed Evan more than twenty-four hours ago, and you're only telling me about this now?" Marisol screeches.

"Sorry!" I say. "It's practically the first time I've seen you since it happened."

"Quiet on the set!" Andrew calls from the other side of the hedges. It turns out "making a documentary" means Andrew spending all afternoon lurking outside the school trying to ask the lunch ladies "hard-hitting" questions about meat loaf and filming them through the windows cooking tomorrow's lunch, while Marisol and I hide out behind bushes in case he needs us to help him.

"Plastic bag!" Andrew calls.

I shoot Marisol a look. "I think it's your turn this time," I say.

She sighs and trots over to remove the offensive plastic bag from the shot. Then she comes to hide next me again so as not to disturb Andrew's view of the side door to the cafeteria. So far, only two lunch ladies have agreed to talk to him, and it was clear the last thing they wanted to talk about was the school's food. "Why did you pick such a boring topic?" one of them even asked. "We've been making the same recipes for twenty years!" Andrew, however, doesn't seem discouraged. He's convinced there's an interesting story here. I hope he's right or else Marisol and I will have to sit through one seriously blah movie.

"Okay. Your first kiss," Marisol whispers. "Tell me everything." For the first time since school started, I feel like I have her undivided attention.

But as I tell her the story, her eyebrows draw closer and closer together. "Wait," she says finally. "You kissed him during gym class? While you were both sweaty from dodgeball? And then you *apologized*?"

It doesn't sound all that great when she puts it like that. "But he said it was nice," I say, and suddenly the doubts I had yesterday at his house start to creep in again.

Marisol frowns. "He hasn't tried kissing you since?"

"Um, no. We haven't had a chance." But that's not really true. We had plenty of chances at his house last night.

"Maybe I did it wrong," I say.

Marisol gives me a sympathetic smile. "I'm sure it's fine. He might have gotten a little spooked, that's all. But if you kiss him again, then—"

"Wait. I have to do it *again*? I thought it was his turn!"

"It's not like tag!" She laughs. "There aren't turns or anything. You do it when it feels right."

I hate how she makes it sound so easy. Seriously, did everyone get a manual on dating except me?

Marisol goes back to scowling at her phone, probably filling out more stuff for Ms. Emerald. I guess that means our conversation is over.

"How long are we supposed to crouch here?" I call over to Andrew. "My butt's falling asleep." Not to mention that the foul odors wafting out of the kitchen are making my stomach turn. It smells more like a chemistry lab than a kitchen. Pierre from the Cooking Club would be happy.

"Only another hour or two!" Andrew calls from behind his camera as he perches outside one of the windows, straining to get a shot of something or other.

I sigh and pull out my phone, thumbing through the Truth Game. I'd been so excited to enter in my bonus points for kissing Evan, but now they feel a little hollow. Still, I go ahead and put in my points for doing something to show my parents how I feel about them. Really I should get double the points since I'm going along with this whole moving idea and I'm going rock climbing with Dad. Sometimes I don't even recognize myself anymore!

Then, just for fun, I write in a part that describes Evan's and my first kiss in the bonus section at the end. When I write it all out, I realize Marisol was right to be horrified. The part about my sweat dripping onto his lip is pretty gross. And I certainly never thought I'd have my first kiss while wearing my too-small sports bra! Okay, so it wasn't perfect, but it counts. Still, I write "Not the kiss first I'd always imagined, but hopefully next time will be better" at the end and hit Submit.

A little while later, Andrew finally releases us from our duties. He heads home to review his footage while I go back to Marisol's house to wait for my mom to pick me up.

Once we settle in on the porch, Marisol is on her phone again.

"Do you want to help me come up with a list of club goals?" she asks.

I groan. "I'm having a hard enough time coming up with one Cooking Club goal for myself. I don't think you really want my help."

She shrugs and goes back to squinting at her phone. I finally tell her she can go on inside and work on her laptop instead of sitting out here with me. "Are you sure?" she says. "It is hard to do all this stuff on a small screen."

"It's fine. Go."

She gives me a little wave and disappears inside. I'm not even annoyed that Marisol is practically ignoring me, just sad that we seem to be on totally different planets these days. Hopefully that will change once the Fashion Club is a done deal.

Since I'm expecting my mom to pick me up, I'm surprised when Mr. Hammond pulls into Marisol's driveway.

"Your mom got held up at work," he says. "Some kind of clogged drain emergency. I hope you don't mind getting a ride with me instead."

"No, that's okay," I say as I climb into the front seat of his little hatchback, although honestly I'm a little weirded out. I've never had to spend an entire car ride alone with Mr. Hammond. If things get really awkward, there's nowhere to hide.

"So how's the bakery job going so far?" he asks, almost like he practiced what to say on the ride over.

"Good. Um, I'm working on some fun ideas for a

birthday cake. I've never used edible glitter before." I don't tell him that other than that detail, I still have no idea what to do for Angela's cake, or that my kitchen is currently covered with a light sprinkling of glitter that even my mom's crazy vacuuming skills haven't been able to defeat, or that I'm not even technically supposed to be working on the cake at all.

He makes a face. "In my day, you only ate glitter by accident!" He gives me a warm smile, and I can't help smiling back. I like Mr. Hammond. If my mom had to choose someone else to be with other than my dad, I really couldn't have picked a nicer guy for her. I only wish this whole situation wasn't so awkward.

"So have you started packing?" he asks.

"Um, no. I didn't realize we were in a rush." My mom told me that she and Mr. Hammond hadn't even talked about a time line for the move yet.

"No, no rush! But if we are going to do it anyway, there's no sense in dragging our feet." Mr. Hammond clears his throat again. "Has your father found a place to live yet?"

"He's still in a hotel, but he has a good job now, so I'm sure he'll be able to find a place soon."

I can almost hear what he's thinking, that my dad is

notorious for quitting perfectly good jobs when he gets tired of them.

"He really wants to stay this time," I say. "He'll find a way to make it work."

"Well, good," Mr. Hammond says. "Then I hope it all turns out the way you're imagining."

I bite back a sigh. That makes two of us.

Chapter 17

Instead of spending my afternoon off hanging out with friends or doing homework like a normal person, I'm in an indoor climbing gym at the foot of a giant wall with about ten pounds of ropes strapped around my body. Meanwhile, my dad is in heaven. He's halfway up the beginner wall already, navigating the fake rocks so effortlessly that I start to wonder if he's part monkey or something while our overly perky instructor, Sheila, cheers him on with each step. "Keep it up, Ted!"

He keeps going and going until he gets to the top. He flashes me a thumbs-up, like being up there is the most natural thing in the world. Then he lets Sheila lower him down, even though it means trusting that his harness will hold him and that he won't fall to the floor like a sack of potatoes.

When he's on solid ground again, Dad starts unhooking his gear. "All right, your turn, Roo!"

"Are you sure you don't want to go again?" I ask, but Sheila is already clipping me in.

"You're all ready to go!" she says a minute later.

"What if I fall?" I say as Dad shoos me toward the foot of the wall.

"Don't worry," Sheila assures me. "We'll catch you."

"But what if I land weird and bang my head against one of the rocks? You weren't there when I almost got a concussion during dodgeball the other day!"

Sheila and my dad both laugh like they think I'm joking. It doesn't look like there's any way I'm getting out of this. And I didn't come all this way and spend all that time strapping myself into harnesses and letting some overly cheerful lady loop about a million ropes around me to turn back now. So I close my eyes, take a deep breath, and take a step forward.

"Way to go, Roo!" Dad says with a hoot.

After I wipe my sweaty hands on my pants, I dust some chalk on my fingers to keep them from slipping. Then I gingerly reach up and grab the first handhold and pull myself up until I can put my other hand a little above my head. Oddly, my foot seems to follow suit so I don't even have to think about where to put it. It simply finds a spot. Huh. Maybe this isn't so bad.

I focus on finding the next handhold, and miraculously there's one right next to me. I transfer my weight so that I can grab it and move my leg up at the same time. I work steadily like that for another couple minutes until I realize that I'm no longer near the ground. In fact, my feet are over my dad's head.

"Great job, Roo!" he says, clearly impressed. That makes two of us. I can't believe that instead of freaking out, I'm actually excited to keep going.

Encouraged, I start going faster. And before I know it, I'm at the top. I can't believe I did it! I almost wish someone had been filming the whole thing so I could show it to Mrs. Da Silva. There's no way she'll believe me without proof.

When I get back on solid ground again, I turn to Sheila and say, "Is there a harder one I can try?"

She looks surprised. "Usually we encourage newbies to stick with this wall for the first couple of climbs."

"But this one was easy. I want to see if I can do a harder one."

"I wouldn't mind trying out a tougher one myself," Dad says.

Sheila finally agrees and leads us over to a wall that slants backward a little. I stare up at it, wondering if I'm really crazy enough to go up, but before I can change my mind, she's already sending me up.

At first, I have no trouble. My arms and legs seem to know exactly what to do again. But after a few minutes, I reach out to grab the next handhold—and miss. Oof! I just manage to avoid falling by grabbing the spot I'd been holding before. I look around, trying to find somewhere else to go, but there isn't anywhere. I'm stuck all the way on the far right of the wall with nowhere to go. There are no handholds that I can reach above my head, and the ones to the left of me seem about a mile away.

"What do I do now?" I call down.

"Try to find another place to put your left foot!" Sheila says.

I try to do what she says, but my limbs suddenly feel shaky, and I can't reach my foot out far enough to get over.

"I'm stuck!" I call.

I glance over at the foothold to my left again. It feels so far away that the only way I'll be able to make it is to jump. I look down at my harness. That's what it's for, isn't it? To catch me in case I don't make it?

I don't let myself look down at the ground. Instead, I

take a deep breath and leap to the left. For a second, I feel the rock under my hands, and I think I've done it. Then it slips out of my grasp, and I plummet through the air. I jerk to a stop as the harness catches me and sends me flailing into the wall.

"Ouch!" I yelp as my elbow scrapes against the fake rock.

"You okay?" Sheila asks as she lowers me to the ground.

I nod, cradling my arm. It stings, but it's not broken or anything. My pride, however, has seen better days.

"Nice job, Roo!" Dad says. "You were so close to the top!"

"But I fell."

Dad looks at me like I've lost my mind. "It was your first time. Did you expect to be perfect right away? Anyway, you were having fun, weren't you?"

I realize that I actually was. "It was like my arms and legs knew where to go!" I say. "I've never felt that coordinated before."

Dad grins. "Maybe we could come back sometime."

And to my surprise, I find myself answering, "Yeah, we definitely should."

Chapter 18

"And, voilà! You have trail mix!" Mrs. Da Silva says. Then she passes around the mix she just "cooked" while Pierre furiously finishes taking notes.

"Is it possible to freeze-dry the ingredients?" he asks.

"Good question!" she says. "How about you research that for next week and let me know." Pierre looks eager to do just that, even though she didn't actually answer his question.

I sigh and take a handful of trail mix to try. It is tasty, but this is not what I signed up for.

"Now, let's get back to working on your goals for the year." Mrs. Da Silva goes to check in with Pierre who's printed out a million pages of instructions on how to make some weird gelatinous fish recipe. Gross.

Then Whit explains the different kid-friendly recipes he's tried out on his nephews and how they still refuse to eat anything he makes.

"Keep at it," Mrs. Da Silva says. "Their taste buds need a chance to adjust." Then she turns to me. "Lee, have you decided what your goal is for the year? Something more specific?"

"I want to get on *Pastry Wars*," I announce. That's nice and specific, isn't it?

"The TV show?"

I nod and tell her about how I auditioned and didn't get in, but how I think I've found a way to get a second chance.

"And what will you get out of being on the show?" she asks.

"Well, hopefully I'd win!" I say. "Then you get scholarship money, which I can use to go to culinary school when I'm older."

"That is a nice perk, but how will it make you a better cook right now?"

"Well, I'd have to prove myself to other people," I say. "And trying to get on the show has me trying all this fancy stuff I wouldn't have made otherwise."

Mrs. Da Silva doesn't look convinced, but she leaves me alone to doodle in my baking journal. I start working on ideas for Angela's cake again, but they all seem silly. Every once in a while, I check my phone to see if there's any word from Chip Ackerson, but so far nothing.

Then my phone beeps, and my heart leaps. But it's not Chip. It's a message from the Truth Game. At first I think it's my daily stats, but then I realize that a list of dozens of names is included. One name catches my eye: Angela Bareli. I click on it, and my mouth drops open when I realize what I'm looking at: the answers to her Truth Game questions! She loves her new cross-country friends, she hates peanut butter, and she's afraid no one will come to her birthday party.

Oh my goldfish. What is this? Some kind of hoax? I scroll through the list of names and see Briana's toward the end. When I click on her answers, I see they're the same things she told me she wrote: getting out of a speeding ticket, cheating on an exam, and so on. This is for real. Somehow, the answers that were supposed to be anonymous are all right here! Hundreds of them. The game must have been hacked!

My stomach goes cold. *Wait. Does that mean…?*

I quickly scroll through and, sure enough, find my name on the list. I click on it and see everything I wrote, about my parents, about Evan, and about Marisol. "Write down one thing no one knows about your best friend." *No. No, no, no, no, no!* What I wrote about Marisol and Andrew is there for everyone to see! Marisol is going to hate me! I start to hyperventilate until I realize that maybe she won't actually see it. If she doesn't play the game, maybe she won't even know about it.

My mind races. Did I write anything about anyone else? Evan. I said that stuff about wishing our first kiss had been better. I hadn't meant it as anything bad, but now that I think about it again, I realize how awful that might sound. Not to mention the fact that I said I didn't know if we'd be together in six months. Gah!

With shaking hands, I look through the names again until I find what I was afraid of: Evan's name. I didn't realize he even played the game, but maybe Briana signed him up for it too.

I skim through his answers, and my chest lightens. Most of them are blank, and the answers he did include are pretty tame. But then I see it, in his questionnaire about relationships. "My girlfriend keeps kissing me and stuff in public. I wish she could take a hint."

The phone slips out of my hand and lands on the counter. I can't believe it. I thought I was being paranoid about Evan not liking me as much as I like him, but I wasn't. In fact, I didn't realize how wrong I was.

* * *

School the next day is a war zone. It turns out Briana was right about lots of kids playing the Truth Game, which means that suddenly everyone knows tons of secrets about each other. I realize that mine aren't nearly as bad as some of the others I've heard about: kids confessing to cheating on tests or on boyfriends and girlfriends, to stealing, and all sorts of other awful stuff. But the worst are the secrets that people told about each other.

I'd stupidly hoped that Marisol wouldn't find out what I said about her, but since word is all around school about the game getting hacked, it didn't take long for Marisol to find out about it. And, not surprisingly, she's not answering any of my messages.

I haven't tried reaching out to Evan, and I haven't heard from him either. I can't believe I thought someone like him could really like someone like me. I'm crushed, but I have to admit that I'm also angry. Because he really made me think that he liked me. And I really like him. And is there really something so wrong with me that he'd hate the idea of kissing me? Am I really so terrible?

I'm not the only one who's walking around fuming. No matter where kids were on the popularity scale, they've been taking down a few notches. And some girl actually bursts into tears during math class and rushes out of the room. I know how she feels.

I don't know whether I should be relieved or even more upset that I don't have gym class today. That means I don't have to face Evan, but it also means I'll have more time to worry about what it will be like to see him tomorrow. Will he actually talk to me? Do I even want him to?

After I have to maneuver around the kissing couple at my locker yet again, I get to lunch to find that Marisol isn't at our usual table. Instead, Andrew is there, scribbling away in a ratty notebook that I know he fills with film notes. When he looks up at me, his thin lips get even thinner.

"Oh. Rachel," he says, not sounding at all glad to see me.

"Is Marisol avoiding me?" I ask.

He sighs. "Yes. It might be best if you don't sit here today."

Just then, I catch a glimpse of Marisol's dark curls in the cafeteria line, and I rush over to her. "Marisol, wait!"

"What do you want?" she asks, paying for her fruit salad.

"I'm sorry! All that stuff I said, I didn't mean it! And I had no idea anyone would find out!"

"Thanks to you, my mom knows about me lying to her

about Andrew. She heard about it from one of her friends whose daughters played that stupid game. And now I'm not allowed to go anywhere after school, not even to meet with Ms. Emerald. I can kiss the Fashion Club good-bye."

"I'm so sorry, Marisol. I never—"

"You know, I started thinking about all the stuff we've been through since we became friends," she says, "and I realized that every big drama in my life has involved you. When you had me make up that stupid fake boy-friend, or when you and I got into that huge fight, or when you had me pull those pranks with you. And after all of that, you say that you're not even sure you want us to be friends?"

"I missed you, that's all. You've been so busy with the club and everything. I missed not having you around."

"So you wished you weren't even friends with me?"

"No! I didn't mean it that way! I've just been—"

"Forget it," she says. Then she turns and storms over to the table to sit with Andrew.

I stand there clinging to my lunch, my body feeling heavier and heavier. If I can't sit with Marisol, then I have nowhere else to go.

Finally, I spot Angela at a table near the door with her

cross-country friends. I drag myself over to her. "Mind if I sit with you?" I whisper, ashamed to have to beg like a stray dog.

"Sure!" she says. Then she introduces me to all the other kids sitting at the table, but I'm barely paying attention. I can't help glancing over at Marisol and Andrew who are hunched over his film notes, chatting away as if nothing is wrong.

"What's going on with you and Marisol?" Angela finally asks. "Is everything okay?"

"Oh, um…" I'm hesitant to say anything since I'm so used to Angela being a huge gossip. But she seems genuinely concerned, so I decide to confide in her a little bit. "She's mad about some of my answers about her in the Truth Game."

"Ugh," Angela says. "I'm so glad I didn't write anything really bad in there. Did you hear some senior broke into a house and stole some stuff and then admitted to it in the game? Now he might go to jail!"

"That's crazy," I say. All of this is crazy. Why did any of us play that stupid game? I want to blame it all on Briana, but the truth is, I was actually kind of having fun playing. It was reassuring to know that my scores weren't so different from other people's. And if it weren't for the game, I probably would never have had my first kiss.

I glance at the clock and see it's almost time for Evan to sneak out of Spanish class and come visit me at lunch. Not that I'm expecting him to, but I can't help watching the door anyway. The minutes tick by, and he doesn't appear in the doorway. My stomach clenches into a tighter and tighter knot.

Just when I give up hope, I see a flash of Evan's Celtics jersey in the doorway. He lingers in the doorway, like he's not sure if he wants to stay. And even though I'm still hurt about what he said, I also can't let things go without at least apologizing to him.

"Evan!" I say, afraid he might keep walking.

But he stops and gives me a little wave. He doesn't say anything though.

"Um, how are you?" I ask, my cheeks suddenly hot.

"All right, I guess." I can't help noticing that he doesn't look me in the eye. "Um, I should get going."

"Wait…I…" I want to apologize, but what's the point? If he really doesn't like me, then what's left to say?

"Really, I should go," he says. Then he turns and hurries back toward his Spanish class.

As I slink back to Angela's lunch table, I can't stop shaking. And I realize it's not only because I'm mad at whoever leaked those answers. I'm also mad at myself. I thought I'd left the old me behind, the one who did and said stupid things that would come back to bite her in the buttons. The idea that I could become a new version of myself was a joke. If anything, trying to be a new me has only caused more trouble than ever before.

Chapter 19

The minute Briana comes into the bakery, she shoots me a look that could easily slice someone in half. That's not unusual for her, but the fact that she's not on her phone tells me something is up.

"What's wrong with you?" I ask. I'm in too foul of a mood to even try to be nice.

"As if you don't know," she says.

"What's that supposed to mean?"

"Oh come on, like you couldn't wait to tell everyone that I worked here the minute you saw me in this stupid apron. I bet you loved seeing the 'queen bee' taken down, right?"

And suddenly I understand why she's so angry. She must have seen the stuff I wrote about her in the Truth Game.

"Thanks to you," she goes on, "Caitlin and Steve and everyone else think I'm a complete loser."

"I didn't even use your name!" I say, but she's glaring at me as she goes to lean against the counter.

"Why do you care so much about people finding out you work here, anyway?" I say. "You're not the first person to ever have a job, you know."

"Just because you don't care about being a freak doesn't mean I have to be happy about it," she spits out. Then she does something I would never, ever, ever expect from Briana in a gazillion years. She starts to cry.

I stare at her in total shock for a second as tears drip from her perfectly mascaraed eyes. And then she turns and runs into the bathroom, pushing past Cherie who's coming out of the kitchen.

"Is she okay?" Cherie asks.

"I don't know." I go to send Evan a message about it, only to realize that he probably doesn't want to talk to me. "I'm sure she'll be fine."

"Well, I have some goodie bags that need filling," Cherie says. "Are you up for it?"

Great. More grunt work. "Can't I help with the cupcakes for this weekend?" Chef Ryan has been working on a crazy cupcake tower for a sweet sixteen party.

"He told me you'd ask about that," she says with a chuckle. "He said he'll let you put the sprinkles on top when he's done. How's that?"

I sigh. It's better than nothing, I guess. I really wish Chip Ackerson would get in touch with me already, but I still haven't heard anything. And if Chef Ryan doesn't let me anywhere near the Montelle-Brennan wedding cake, then I really might miss my chance.

When Cherie's gone, I hesitate for a second and then pick up the phone and dial the Town Center Inn. I cross my fingers that the old lady I saw the other day answers, and I'm in luck!

"Um, hi," I say. "I don't know if you remember me, but I dropped off some pastries for one of your, um, lodgers the other day."

"Oh yes, for Mr. Ackerson. He said he quite enjoyed them."

"He did?" I almost shriek. "Did he say anything else?"

"No…" she says slowly. "He did seem a little confused about the whole thing, but then he said it had to be the universe telling him he was on the right path."

Oh my goldfish. Chip Ackerson believes in that kind of stuff too!

The old woman laughs. "I guess when you spend most of your life staring into a crystal ball, you should know a thing or two about life's many paths."

I pause. "Crystal ball?" Is Chip into that kind of stuff and I had no idea? It's never been mentioned in any of the articles I've read about him.

"Yes, that's what people like him do, isn't it? Crystal balls, tarot cards, that sort of thing. I imagine they have pretty much everything at that convention of his."

"Convention?" I echo, remembering how she'd mentioned one when I'd been at the inn the other day. "He's here for a convention?"

"Yes, a spirituality and healing one, I think it's called. A lot of New Age nonsense, if you ask me, but his business seems to be doing well, so good for him."

"His business?" I ask, feeling like a parrot.

"Yes, he sells crystals, the healing-energy kind, I guess. He tried to sell me one, but I told him that at my age it's too late for any of that."

"Are you talking about Chip Ackerson?" I say.

"No, no," she says. "Not Chip. Chet. Chet Ackerson. Wait, I thought you knew him. Isn't that why you brought those pastries over?"

I close my eyes, defeat slowly creeping through my entire body. "I guess I was wrong," I say.

* * *

"What are you doing here?" Marisol demands when she opens her front door.

"Did you really see Chip Ackerson at the grocery store, or were you playing a prank on me?"

She blinks at me, obviously surprised. "Yeah, I saw him. Why would I lie about that?" She snorts. "Oh wait, I'm not as honest as I seem, right? Isn't that what you said about me?"

"Marisol, I'm serious. Was it him?" I hold up my phone and show her a picture of Chip. She studies it for a second, and her dark eyebrows knit together.

"It looked like him," she says slowly, "but the guy I saw had more gray hair. And...well, maybe his nose was a little different."

I let out a long breath. "And when you called hotels, who did you ask for?"

She looks at me like I'm crazy. "I told you, I asked around for Chet Ackerson. What's going on? You say all that stuff about me in your stupid game, and now you show up and start grilling me about Chet?"

"Chip!" I cry. "It's Chip Ackerson! Not Chet! The guy you found is some healing-crystal salesman. I knew it was weird that he'd be staying at that inn, but I figured you were trying to help me, so why would I doubt what you said?"

"I *was* trying to help you!" Marisol says. "I feel like all I do is try to help you, and it's never good enough."

"What are you talking about? You spend all your time focused on the Fashion Club or on Andrew. You don't even care what's been going on with me."

"Are you kidding? That's all I hear about! 'Chip has to know what a great cook I am. What recipe should I make for Chip? Do you think I'll ever get on TV?' Since when do you care about that kind of stuff? And the minute I ask you for help, you tell me you're too busy."

"That's not true!"

"I asked you to pick out fabric with me and to help me come up with club goals and stuff, and you were so busy thinking about getting on TV that you just brushed it off."

I want to deny it, but I can't. Because she's right. "But you don't understand. I've been so—"

"Not everything is about you, Rachel!" Marisol cries. "Don't you get that?" Then she does something I would never, ever expect of my best friend. She slams the door in my face.

Chapter 20

When I go to meet my dad at his new job at the canoe shop, I find him inside a huge box truck unloading kayak after kayak with one of the younger guys who works at the store.

"I'll be with you in a minute, Rachel Roo," my dad says. "Only thirty more to go!" He has a huge grin on his face, as if he's having a great time, even though I can tell by how filthy and sweaty he is that he's been doing this for at least an hour. The guy he's working with looks at him like he's insane.

As I sit in the corner of the shop, my phone beeps. It's a new message from Mom. Robert said we can start bringing things over this weekend.

Before I know it, a couple of tears have trickled down my cheeks.

"Ready to go get some dinner?" Dad asks. Then he must see my face because he rushes over. "Roo, what's wrong?"

I can't exactly pretend that nothing is wrong, so I tell him about Marisol and Evan being mad at me and about the stupid mix-up with Chip-Chet. "And on top of all that," I say, "I thought I was okay with the whole moving thing, but now I'm not so sure."

Over the summer, I even told my mom that she should go ahead and look for apartments for us since it was getting harder for her to pay our mortgage. But after her cleaning business merged with Ladybug Cleaners, it looked like we might be able to stay in the house after all. Now I have to get used to the idea of moving all over again.

"Oh, I know, Roo," Dad says, putting his arm around me even though he's covered in grime. "You've never been that great with change."

His words make me feel better, but it's not because of his sympathy. It's because I realize that I'm being my old self, the one who was afraid of changing the way she cut her caramel squares because she'd always done it a certain way. But new-and-improved me isn't afraid of new things. I mean, she climbed a wall! That means she can deal with moving too, right?

"I'll get over it," I say, wiping my eyes. "And my room

at Mr. Hammond's house is going to be twice the size of my room now. That's definitely a plus."

"There you go," Dad says as we head over to his car. "And if it makes you feel any better, I looked at an apartment down the street from our—ahem, I mean, *your mom's* house. So if I wind up getting it, you'll at least be in the same neighborhood when you come stay with me."

"You did? No more living in a hotel?" I ask, getting into the passenger seat.

"Nope!" Dad says. "And the place has a nice big kitchen, so you'll have plenty of room to bake your amazing creations."

I sigh. "I don't know how amazing they are. I'm supposed to be working on a birthday cake for Angela Bareli's birthday party, but I can't come up with any good ideas."

"What have you tried so far?"

I list off the different ideas I had, but all of them seem so boring. "I feel like I need to do something really big, you know? Something that people won't be able to miss."

"You know, I feel like I've spent years trying to find something big," he says. "Switching jobs, moving to Florida. But all it did was make me realize that the stuff that mattered to me was the everyday, ordinary stuff."

"Are you calling me ordinary?" I tease.

He tugs on my ear. "You? Never. All I'm saying is, maybe you don't always have to go for something over-the-top to make a big impression."

That sounds nice, but Dad doesn't get it. Angela's party is going to be as over-the-top as it gets. The cake has to match it. And I have to come in with a cake that blows Chef Ryan's cake out of the water, one that Angela will definitely choose. But maybe Dad is right. Maybe if I put a few boring things together, I might wind up with something interesting.

● ● ●

I spend the next few days furiously testing out ideas for Angela's cake. I even try an ants on a log–inspired cake just in case Mrs. Da Silva is secretly a genius. (Verdict: dis-gus-ting!)

At least focusing on Angela's cake helps distract me from the fact that Marisol and Evan may never speak to me again. I've tried calling and texting and emailing Marisol, but she hasn't been responding to any of my messages. And the one time I got up the courage to call Evan, I hung up before he answered. He must have seen that he had a missed call from me, but I haven't heard back.

Ugh. I can't think about that right now. Cake first. Personal crisis second.

Finally, the morning of Angela's party, I finish the cake and step back, admiring my work. It's huge and sparkly and the definition of over-the-top. It's covered with flowers and bows and candy, and I even hung a few streamers from the bottom and stuck a shiny birthday hat on top. You can't get any more little kid birthday party than this, and I know Angela is going to die when she sees it.

"That looks like it should be in a magazine!" Mom says when she spots the final product sitting on the counter. "Or in an art museum!"

"Mom," I say, rolling my eyes, but I can't help smiling at the compliment. Even though it felt like torture getting to this point, I'm excited to show the cake to Chef Ryan. Yes, he might be mad at me for going behind his back, but when he sees how right I was about Angela's cake, he'll definitely have me assist him with the Montelle-Brennan cake. He'd be crazy not to.

"Can you help me get it over to the bakery?" I ask. "Angela is going to be there in an hour."

Mom nods. "As long as you don't mind stopping at

Robert's house on the way back. I wanted to measure his living room to see if our couch will fit."

I swallow. The thought of our furniture sitting in someone else's living room still makes me a little sick to my stomach, but I force myself to smile and say, "Sure."

We oh-so-carefully slide the cake into the back of Mom's minivan. I'd put it in a large box, and now I stuff blankets and pillows all around it so there's no way it can get wrecked. When we get to the bakery, Mom helps me carry it inside. It feels like we're transporting the Crown Jewels instead of baked goods, but I'm so glad that Mom understands how important it is for this cake to get there in perfect condition.

"I'm going to run to the bank," Mom says. "Good luck!" she adds in a whisper before ducking outside.

"Rachel, what are you doing here?" Chef Ryan asks when he sees me. "Isn't it your day off?"

"I'm dropping off a cake I made for a client," I say, trying to pretend it's the most natural thing in the world.

He raises a thick eyebrow. "Come again?"

"Um, Angela Bareli is doing a little-kid birthday party, right?" I rush to explain. "And she was worried that your cake might not be right for it, so I thought I'd go ahead and make a second cake just in case, as a backup, you know? In case she liked mine better and wanted to use it."

He stares at me for a long moment. Then his nostrils flare, and he opens the box. He's totally silent as he examines it. Then he says, "It's good."

I let out a breath. He likes it. He actually likes it!

Chef Ryan starts to say something else, but at that moment, Angela bursts into the bakery and gasps when she sees my cake on the counter. "Is that mine?" she shrieks and then starts bouncing around the bakery as she gushes about the colors and the frosting. "It's amazing!" Then her smile dims a little. "Although…it seems a little…busy. Like, my eye doesn't really know where to look. Is there any way we could, I don't know, take a couple things off?"

I swallow. "Maybe the streamers?" I pull them off and hide them behind my back, but Angela's still frowning. "And maybe the cake topper?" I add as I yank the party hat off.

"That's better," she says, but her forehead is still lined. "And maybe…" She chews on her lip for a second. "We could take off some of the flowers or something?"

It took me forever to make the flowers, and now she wants to take them off? But the customer is always right.

Before I can destroy the cake any more though, Chef Ryan turns to Angela and says, "Hold on a second. I want to show you something." He goes into the back room and emerges a minute later with another cake box. When he opens it, Angela gasps as she looks at the perfectly smooth frosting and the tastefully arranged pink and purple flowers.

"That's it!" she yells. "I can't believe it. Did you guys make two cakes for me to choose from because you knew I was so nervous about it being perfect? That's amazing!"

After Chef Ryan's cake is loaded in Mrs. Bareli's car, Angela gives me a big hug and says, "Thank you, Rachel! I'll see you at the party tonight, okay?"

I nod and manage a smile, but the last thing I feel like doing is celebrating.

When Angela's gone, Chef Ryan gets very quiet. I notice his lips are so straight, you could use them as a ruler. He's usually hard to read, but this is stoic even for him. I can't tell if he's proud of me or about to announce that I'm fired.

"What were you thinking, Rachel?" he finally asks in an odd, quiet voice. "Going behind my back like that?"

"I-I was trying to help," I say, but of course that's not

quite true. I was trying to impress him, even if it meant bending the rules a little bit. I guess my new self couldn't quite shake my old self's bad habits.

"You've been asking me to let you help with big projects, but how can I do that? Especially after this? I was going to start training you for some more responsibilities, but now I think that will have to wait until you can prove to me that you can be trusted."

"But…but Angela's cake was good! You said so yourself! It was exactly what she asked for."

"It was good," Chef Ryan says, "but it wasn't your best work. I didn't see your skill and your passion in it."

"My passion?"

"That's why Angela wasn't completely satisfied. It lacked finesse. It was good, but it wasn't great. It didn't feel like you."

"But…but…" I try to object, but I realize he's right. Normally when I'm baking, inspiration hits and I make something that I'm really excited about. This time, I focused on something that fit the theme, something bigger and crazier than anything I would have normally made.

"I know you can do excellent work, Rachel. That's why I'm pushing you to get the basics down cold. Once you have those under your belt and you know your own limits, you'll be a fine baker."

I know I should be glad that he's trying to help, but I've already come so far and it's still not good enough. At this rate, it feels like I'll never get to where I want to be.

Chapter 21

When I get to Angela's birthday party that night, it's even more extravagant than I'd imagined. Her entire house is decked out like a kids' wonderland complete with pony rides, face painting, and not one but *two* bouncy castles. I should be excited to be here. After all, when I was little, no one invited me to their birthday parties because they didn't even remember that I existed. But being here by myself doesn't feel much better. I know Marisol and Evan are both in the crowd, but since neither of them is speaking to me right now, that's not much comfort.

Clearly, I'm not the only one who's uncomfortable. I spot lots of kids who look lost or are talking to people they don't seem to actually like. I wonder if other people's relationships got totally messed up, thanks to the Truth Game. I don't know if that thought makes me feel better or worse.

I position myself near the cotton candy lady—yup,

Angela actually hired someone to make cotton candy!—
and scan the crowd. After a minute I spot Evan talking to
some guy from our gym class. He's laughing and gesturing
like he's reenacting something that happened during volleyball. I know that if I walked up to him though, his smile
would immediately fade.

Part of me wishes that the tingly feeling I get in my
stomach at the sight of him would go away, but another
part of me wishes we could rewind time and go back to
when we first admitted we liked each other. If I did it all
over again, maybe I could find a way to make him still like
me, and I'd definitely think twice before saying anything
bad about him, anonymous or not. But, of course, that's
not an option.

I turn away and spot Angela making the rounds, looking more confident than I've ever seen her.

"Rachel, you came!" she says when she sees me.
"Everyone's been raving about how pretty the cake looks. I
can't wait to eat it!"

"I wanted to come by and wish you a happy birthday. I
can't stay though."

"But you have to at least stick around until I cut the
cake!" she says.

I let her bustle me inside the house and into the kitchen where her mom is putting candles on top of the cake. Now that I'm looking at it again, I can see how much more polished it looks than my gaudy monstrosity. Chef Ryan's cake is like a cherry on top of a great party. My cake would have been like a paint-filled water balloon.

After we sing to Angela and watch her blow out her candles, she comes over to me, still gushing. "You did such an amazing job," she says. "I'm so glad you were at the bakery when I went in! I doubt Briana would have been all that helpful."

I look at her in surprise until I remember about the Truth Game answers. "So I guess you heard Briana works with me?"

Angela gives me a conspiratorial smile. "I'm the one who told people," she says. "I saw her hiding behind the counter when I came to order my cake." She laughs. "As if she could hide that kind of secret for long! You should have seen how shocked Caitlin was when I told her."

"Wait...you're the one who told Caitlin? I thought people found out about it because of what I wrote in the Truth Game."

"Nope! Those answers got leaked on the same day I

told Caitlin, but people would have found out without that game."

"But why would you do that? What do you care if Briana works at a bakery?"

"Because she's always thought she was so much better than everyone else. But now she has a job like a normal person. Besides, it was way too good of a secret to keep to myself."

I shake my head. For weeks I've thought Angela was a new version of herself, but I guess in some weird way Briana was right. Maybe people never completely change. I thought I could leave my old self behind, but middle school Rachel seems to follow me wherever I go, no matter what I do.

Angela's party is suddenly the last place I want to be, so I hurry out the door and wind my way through some jugglers. I swing around a bush at the top of the driveway and smack right into Briana.

"Ow!" she cries, rubbing her shoulder. "What's your problem?"

"You are!" I say.

She rolls her eyes. "What are you even talking about?"

"You want to know who spilled your secret about the

bakery? It was Angela. And because of that stupid game you signed me up for, Evan and Marisol are mad at me."

"Hey, I didn't say that stuff about them. You did. It's not my fault if you feel guilty. And seriously, get over it. Some people have real problems."

"What do you know about real problems?" I snap. "All you care about is making sure you don't miss your next manicure appointment. Evan is working his butt off to help your family, and you spend all your time at the bakery not lifting a finger!"

"I'm not like you, okay? I'm not one of those people who just know how to do stuff. You were probably mopping the floor since you were born. I'd never even touched a mop before I started working at that place. And no one would show me how to use it! You think I like looking like a moron all the time? On top of already feeling like a total loser?"

I can only stare at Briana for a second. Did those words really come out of her mouth? "What do *you* have to feel like a loser about?"

Her eyes just about double in size. "Are you kidding me? I used to rule our grade, our whole school! And then I get dumped by my boyfriend and my best friend on the same day, and then my dad loses his job and I'm suddenly living in some gross Cinderella story where I have to take trash out and stuff. No one at school even cares about me anymore, and most of my old friends totally ignore me. I mean, Angela Bareli is more popular than I am now. Do you know what that's like, to think Angela Bareli's life is better than yours?"

And the funny thing is, I do know. Because on the first day of school, when everything was going wrong, I was jealous of Angela for having her life together. But it turns out she's still the same old person she was in middle school, just with a better hobby.

"It doesn't matter anyway," Briana says. "I'm not making nearly enough money at the bakery."

"For what, your fancy clothes?" I say.

"No, for Evan's tuition," she says, lowering her voice even though I doubt anyone can hear us over the blaring music from Angela's house. "God, do you really think I'm that shallow?"

"You're working to help Evan save up for school next year?"

"Yeah, so?"

"But…but why would you do that? You guys aren't exactly close."

"He's still my brother," she says like I'm a total idiot for not understanding. Then she pushes past me and goes inside Angela's house.

As I watch her disappear, it occurs to me that just because Angela is the same as she ever was doesn't mean that the rest of us have to be. I might make some of the same old mistakes, but I know I've changed for the better over the past few months. Maybe that means Briana can too.

My phone rings. It's Cherie calling. That's weird. Why would she be calling me on a Friday night?

"Rachel, I need your help," she says when I answer the phone. "Ryan is in the hospital."

"Oh my goldfish! Is he okay? What happened?"

"He'll be all right. He was watering the herbs in the bakery, and he fell off the ladder and broke his leg and his collarbone." She lets out a long breath. "I can't believe this is happening the day before our biggest wedding! That means I need you to finish the cake."

"You need me to *what*?"

"It's almost done, but my husband can't put the finishing touches on it. I'll need you to do it. Can you come in early tomorrow morning and handle it? I'll let you inside at seven before I head over to the venue with the other girls to set up."

I swallow. This is it. The pineapple gods are finally answering my prayers and giving me a chance to show everyone what I can do. "I'll be there," I tell her.

Chapter 22

In the morning, I arrive at the bakery with my whole body jiggly with nerves. I tried to find my lucky shirt again—the one that I couldn't wear on the first day of school because I managed to stain it with toothpaste—but it seems to have disappeared for good. I guess I'll have to get through what could be the Most Important Day of My Life without it.

Cherie assures me that Chef Ryan is going to be okay and says that they're both counting on me. Then she says she'll be back to pick up the cake at noon and runs out the door, leaving me standing alone in the bakery.

I'm frozen for a second, suddenly terrified. Then I tell myself to pull it together, and I go into the kitchen to check out the Montelle-Brennan cake. The three tiers are all frosted, but they still need to be put together and decorated in the intricate pattern of iced roses that Chef

Ryan sketched out. Even though I'm still not convinced the design is perfect for the occasion—it looks a little too stuffy and uptight—it's beautiful. And after Angela's cake, I'm not about to start questioning his vision. I only need to assemble the cake and make the roses to go on top, and it'll be done. And hey, that means a tiny bit of my work will wind up on TV, even if I wish it had happened a different way.

Okay. I can do this.

I riffle around in the supply cabinets—careful not to make a mess so Chef Ryan doesn't freak out when he comes back—and gather what I need. Then I get to work. Since the cake has to be put together for the roses to go on it, I decide to assemble it first. I've never worked on a cake this big before. From what I've heard, a lot of bakeries assemble their cakes at the wedding location and finish the decorating there, but I don't think we have time for that. I'll have to put it together here and hope that it makes the trip in one piece. I'm sure Cherie can do a little bit of touch-up work at the venue if need be.

I take a deep breath and carefully lift the second tier and place it on the bottom one. Then, holding my breath again, I pick up the smallest tier and gently place it on top.

I realize, too late, that I should have measured out the tiers before putting them together, but even eyeballing it, they come out pretty good. The top tier might be a tiny bit off-center, but it won't be all that noticeable once I put the roses on it.

I'm sweating like crazy from the stress, so I hurry to the bathroom to splash cold water on my face before I start on the roses. When I come back out, I glance at the clock and see I still have more than four hours before Cherie comes to pick up the cake. At this rate, I'll be done in way less time than that!

Thankfully, Chef Ryan already made the colored fondant, so I only have to shape it and put it on the cake. Roses look impressive, but they're actually pretty easy to make. I shape the petals and then carefully wrap them around each other until they start to look like blooming roses. I put them on wires so they'll be easy to put into the cake without worrying about them falling off.

When I've made a half dozen of the roses, I peek at the cake to see how it's doing—

"Oh my goldfish!" I shriek.

Half of the middle layer is caving in on itself! The cake is collapsing!

I run around the kitchen, frantically looking for something I can use to keep the cake from sagging more, and find a bunch of dowels that I shove into the tiers. But when I try to reshape the cake, it's no use. The middle layer is completely sagging, and the bottom one is collapsing too. No amount of frosting will cover that up.

I don't get it. What did I do wrong?

And then I look at the dowels again and remember something I saw on TV a long time ago about stabilizing wedding cakes with wooden or hollow plastic dowels to keep them from caving in. Since Chef Ryan usually assembles cakes on-site, I've never seen him do it before, but that must be how he keeps his cakes from collapsing. In my rush to put it together, I hadn't even thought about reinforcing it! Why didn't I ask Chef Ryan about that kind of stuff instead of badgering him to let me put vines on things? It doesn't matter if a cake has fancy decorations on it if it's falling apart!

Gah! The cake needs to be at the venue in less than four hours, and it's a total mess! What am I supposed to do?

Tears start stinging my eyes, but I push them back. There's no time for crying right now. I grab my phone and call Cherie, but there's no answer. She's probably off taking care of some other wedding emergency. I think about leaving her a message, but I don't want her to freak out. So instead, I call my mom even though I know she's busy at work.

"Okay, don't panic," Mom says after I explain what happened, but it's a little late for that. Her voice is echoey which probably means she's cleaning someone's bathroom.

"I can't believe I did this! No matter what I do, I always mess things up and drag everyone else into it!"

"Honey, stop beating yourself up," Mom says. "Yes, you make mistakes, but you always fix them."

"But I don't want to always fix my messes!" I say. "I want to not make them in the first place!" I'm so mad at myself that the tears start trying to pour out again.

"That would be impossible," Mom says.

"I know, I know. I'll always make a mess. That's just who I am."

"No. You're a human. That means you can't help but be imperfect. But that also means you can find a way to make things right."

For some reason, I think about rock climbing with my dad and how I decided to actually leap through the air and risk falling to the ground rather than climb back down and try to fix my mistakes. I thought I was being brave and pushing myself to do big stuff, but maybe if I'd slowed down and actually focused on learning the basics first, I wouldn't have fallen at all. "You've got to crawl before you can walk," Chef Ryan keeps saying, and I keep rolling my eyes, but maybe he's right. And part of crawling is falling on your face over and over, until you finally learn what you're doing.

"Okay. I have to go."

"Do you want me to come help you?" Mom says. "You don't have to do this on your own."

"I know," I say, "but you're busy. I'll be okay."

"Are you sure? I can tell my clients I have to reschedule. I can—"

"No, really. It's my mess, and I'll figure it out. You have your own stuff to worry about."

"Okay." I can hear the reluctance in her voice. But she promised to let me handle my own problems from now on, and I guess she's keeping her word. She tells me to call if I need anything, and then she hangs up.

As I stand there staring at the destroyed cake, I know I need to start over and make a new one. It seems crazy and impossible, but it's the only way. And my mom is right. I'm going to need some help.

Chapter 23

"What do you mean you're making slime?" I say into the phone.

"It's not slime," Pierre corrects me. "It's sludge. I have made an oil sludge that I plan to transform into a—"

"You can't put your sludge project on hold for a few hours and come help me? I'm really, really desperate." He's a foodie like I am. That means he can't ignore a food emergency, right? It's like foodie code or something.

I hear some kind of alarm go off in the background. "Oh, my mixture is ready. Sorry, Rachel. But good luck." Then he hangs up.

I groan and reluctantly call Whit. After a few rings, he picks up, but the noise in the background is so deafening that I can barely hear him.

"Where are you?" I ask.

"At the arcade with my nephews," he yells into the

phone. "Sorry, it's really loud in here. Can I call you back?"

"Actually, I need your help!" I try to explain to him about the cake, but I can tell he still can't hear me.

"I'll see you at school, okay? We're going to get some food. I actually convinced them to eat grilled cheese! I know it's not the kind of stuff Mrs. Da Silva wants us eating, but it's better than Cheetos, right?" Then the phone cuts out. I can't tell if he hung up on me or if we got disconnected, but either way, I'm on my own.

I sink into a chair, my face in my hands. Now what do I do? I thought the whole point of being in a cooking club was to be around "my people," but how can they be my people when I can't even count on them in an emergency?

But then I realize. I do have people like that. They might not know much about wedding cakes, and they might hate my guts right now, but I'd do anything for them. Hopefully that means they'll do anything for me.

● ● ●

"Thank you guys for coming," I say. "I know I totally don't deserve your help, but—"

"Just tell us what you want us to do," Marisol says. "There's not a lot of time."

"Yeah," Evan adds. "Whatever you need, we'll do it."

I could hug them and cry, but there's no time for that. Amazingly, it took almost no convincing to get them here. I sent SOSes to both of them, and within a few minutes, they were on their way. All the stuff that happened between us isn't gone, not by a long shot, but right now it doesn't matter, not when there's so much we have to do.

While I was waiting for them to get to the bakery, I came up with a game plan. Since Marisol is a terrible cook but a great artist, she's going to help me with the decorating. Evan is pretty good at cooking on the other hand, so he's going to help me bake the cake.

"We're remaking the cake exactly the way it was?" Marisol asks.

"No," I say, and they both stare at me in shock. "I can't make it the same way he did. I don't know how." It hurts to admit that, but it's true. When I took this job, I thought I was as good as Chef Ryan, maybe even better. But the truth is, I have a lot to learn. "Ms. Montelle said she totally trusted Chef Ryan to do whatever he thought would work. She wanted the cake to be a surprise. So we're making one I know will be perfect. Even if it won't be nearly as fancy."

I only hope Chef Ryan won't murder me with a whisk when he finds out what I've done.

Marisol nods. "Okay, so what do we do instead?"

"We can keep the same flavors, but it should look more like…" I hurry over and grab a piece of paper. Then I start sketching what I've had in my head since I first heard about the wedding.

As I make my pitiful sketch, Marisol adds a few touches to help clarify what I'm thinking. When we're done, it's perfect. And, unlike when I was making Angela's cake, I can feel the excitement pulsing through me. Chef Ryan might fire me for messing up his cake and making a totally different one, but if I have to start all over, I'm going to make a cake that I'm passionate about, one that feels like me, like he said.

"Thank you," I tell Marisol. "Really. I don't know what I'd do without you."

I hope she can see how much I mean it, but she just shrugs and says, "Let's get to work." Then she goes off in the corner. Clearly, she's still mad at me, but she's also my best friend. That means getting me out of yet another jam even though I probably don't deserve her help.

Meanwhile, Evan's already started gathering ingredients

for the cake. Since we don't have time to make more fondant to cover the cake, I start making a buttercream frosting instead. I can practically feel the clock ticking, but I try to take a deep breath. If we keep our heads down and keep working, we might be able to pull this off.

Once the cake layers are baked and cooling and the buttercream frosting is done, I glance over at Evan and realize he's covered in flour and sugar and icing. Despite it all, he looks absolutely adorable.

"What?" he says when he catches me looking at him.

"Um, nothing," I say. "I just… Thank you for being here. I know you're still mad at me, and I know things are really weird between us right now, but I really appreciate it."

He nods and wipes his forehead with the back of his hand. "Did you mean it?" he asks after a minute. "What you said in the game about us not being together in six months?"

"No!" I say. "I *wanted* us to be together that long. I hoped we would be. It felt like jinxing the whole thing if I said we definitely would be, you know? I thought things were going really well, but I guess they weren't."

"They weren't?" he says, sounding surprised. "I thought they were."

"You did? But…but you said you didn't want me touching you in public. You said I couldn't take a hint!"

He looks down at the floor, suddenly looking embarrassed. "I've never been good with PDAs. I mean, look at my family. The only time my parents even hold hands is when they're at some big charity event and they want to prove to everyone how happy they are. I liked kissing you and stuff." He blushes. "But I wish it had been when other people weren't around, you know?"

"Wait, so you…so you still like me?"

He looks at me like I've lost my mind. "Of course I still like you. Why wouldn't I?" He gives me a hopeful look. "Do you still like me?"

"Are you kidding? Of course I do!"

We stand there in giddy silence for a second. Then I smile as I notice a glob of frosting on his shirt. "You have a little something on you."

He glances down at his filthy clothes and laughs. "I guess I do. And you…" He takes a step forward and smears some frosting on my cheek. "You have a little something on you too."

And that's when it happens. He leans forward and I lean forward, and our lips find each other. And then I swear angels start singing! I close my eyes and feel the warmth of his lips on mine. And there's no sweat or gym sock smell this time. There are just his lips pressed against mine, and the tiniest hint of powdered sugar.

Finally, we pull away, and I find Evan looking back at me with a question in his eyes.

"Well?" he says. "Was that any better than last time?"

I'm tempted to bury my face in my hands from embarrassment, but I'm still on too much of a kissing high. "The first time was perfect because it was with you," I say. "And this time was perfect too. I was an idiot for saying anything else. I'm sorry."

He smiles and dabs some more frosting on my chin. "Don't worry about it, Booger Crap." Then he leans in and kisses me again, and that's how I know I'm really forgiven.

• • •

Two hours later, the cake is done. The three of us stand there staring at it in awe.

"It's perfect," Marisol whispers, and I have to agree. The pale-yellow buttercream frosting looks light and fluffy, the tiers are securely fastened with plastic dowels, and the blue and white shells and starfish that Marisol made out of the leftover fondant are subtle yet stunning.

The whole thing screams waterfront wedding, and I know Ms. Montelle will love it. I only hope Chef Ryan feels the same way.

We carefully box up the cake and wait for Cherie to arrive. I sit there holding Evan's hand. Or he's holding mine. It doesn't matter. I was so busy worrying about it all before that I guess I wasn't letting things happen naturally.

"Okay," Marisol say. "I should get going."

"Oh." It's stupid to feel disappointed. Why would she stick around until Cherie gets here? It's not her job that's on the line. "Well, thank you. For everything. Really."

She nods. "No problem."

Before she can walk away, I grab her arm. "Are we...are we ever going to be okay?"

She sighs. "Probably," she says. "But I think I need more time." Then she hops on her bike and rides away.

"She'll come around," Evan says as I watch her disappear around the corner.

"I hope so."

At exactly noon, Cherie pulls up in front of the bakery, her face red. "You weren't answering your phone!" she says. "I saw you called. Is everything okay?"

I realize I didn't even glance at my phone after we got

to work on the cake. "Um, there was a minor crisis, but we figured it out."

"Oh good," she says. "Because we need to pack up the cake and get going."

Evan jumps up to help, and together he and Cherie put it in the back of her catering van. I hold my breath the whole time, but it goes in without a problem.

I expect Cherie to speed off and tell me to keep an eye on the bakery, but instead she turns to me and says, "Grab your supplies and hop in."

"My supplies?" I say.

"If the cake needs any last-minute touching up, you're going to be the one to do it. I won't have time."

"But what about the bakery? Who's going to watch it?"

"We can shut down for one day. If all goes well today, we'll have a lot more business from now on. Now go get your things."

I nod and hurry inside to get some extra tools and supplies. Evan helps me pack everything up and walks me back out to Cherie's van.

We stand there for a minute looking at each other, but for once I don't feel awkward about saying good-bye to him.

"Thank you," I say for probably about the tenth time. "I really owe you."

"Don't worry about it," he says. "Just remember me when you're a famous TV chef, okay?"

I laugh and give him a peck on the cheek. Then I hop into the passenger seat of Cherie's van, and we speed off to the wedding and to what might finally be my big TV debut.

Chapter 24

When we get to the lake, the place is crawling with people even though there's still an hour before the wedding starts. A tent is set up right by the water for the reception, and the end of the dock is blanketed with flowers for the ceremony. The whole scene is stunning and definitely fit for a TV special. And *my* cake is going to be part of it!

Even though I expect Chef Ryan to be home recuperating, I spot him in the food tent in a wheelchair, yelling at people. Briana is rushing around like a wind-up toy. The only other time I've seen her move with such urgency is when she's playing softball.

"What are you doing here?" Cherie cries when she sees her husband. "You're supposed to be at home in bed!"

But he ignores her and says, "I could have finished the cake if I had to. I don't care what the doctor says." He turns to me. "Did everything come out okay?"

My stomach clenches into a ball. "It came out great," I say slowly. "But...it's not exactly the cake you planned."

"What are you talking about?"

"I-it's better if you just see it."

With Chef Ryan barking orders, we unload the cake so carefully that you'd think it was a bomb or something. But when we get it to the food tent and unpack it, I'm relieved to see that it barely needs any touching up at all.

When I look up, I find Chef Ryan staring at the cake with his nostrils flared so widely, they might split apart. He doesn't say a word. Meanwhile, Cherie's eyebrows are practically in her ponytail.

"Um, there was kind of an accident," I try to explain. "And...um..."

"What is this?" Chef Ryan finally says through his teeth. "What did you do?"

"The first cake collapsed...and I was going to redo it exactly the same...but then I realized I didn't know how, so then I thought...the water...the colors..." As the words come out in bursts, I can barely breathe. I can see it in Chef Ryan's eyes. He's going to kill me. Despite his broken bones, he's going to grab a cake knife, slice me into pieces, and serve me for dessert.

I back away a couple steps, ready to make a run for it, when I hear: "Wow, that's a great-looking cake!"

I know that voice. I've heard it a million times in my living room.

I whirl around to find none other than Chip Ackerson standing behind me, studying my handiwork with a huge grin on his face. "It's perfect for the venue," he adds. Then he pats Chef Ryan on the back—on his nonbroken side—and congratulates him on a job well done.

"Not mine," Chef Ryan says. "Hers."

"Why, hello there," Chip say, turning to me. "You're the one responsible for this cake?"

"Oh my goldfish!" I shriek. "It's Chip Ackerson!"

Oh my goldfish! Did I just say that out loud?

"I see we have a young fan." Chip chuckles and shakes my hand, which I'm sure feels sticky from all the leftover frosting still on it. "I'm Chip. And you are?"

"Chip," I say.

He frowns. "Your name is Chip too?"

I shake my head. I want to tell him what a huge fan I am. I want to beg him to put me on his TV show. But all I can say is "Chip" again. What the Shrek is wrong with me? This is my big chance to talk to my idol, and I've turned into a parrot! And then what he said about my handiwork finally sinks in, and that pulls me out of my stupor. "Do you really like my cake?" I ask.

He nods. "I like what you did with the blue starfish. Not an obvious choice, but it works." Then he starts asking me about the flavors, and I tell him that I used the ones Chef Ryan picked out: German chocolate for the bottom tier, cookies and cream for the second tier, and red velvet for the third tier, all covered with rich vanilla buttercream frosting.

"So this wasn't the original design?" Chip asks me.

I laugh and shake my head. "Actually, the first cake kind of fell apart thanks to me. I'd never worked on such a big cake before." Then I tell him the whole story. Now that I'm rehashing it, I realize it's actually kind of funny, even though it certainly didn't feel that way at the time. And even though I'm kind of freaking out about talking to my idol, it's surprisingly easy to tell him about my cake, maybe because I'm so excited about it.

"And this is the end result!" Chip says. "Let that be a handy tip for you viewers at home. Always have the proper support for your cakes. Thanks for telling us about it!"

Wait. Viewers at home?

I turn to find that there's a cameraman standing about five feet away from me and pointing a microphone in my direction. Oh my goldfish! Everything I said was just taped for TV? I was so busy focusing on the cake and on getting potentially murdered by Chef Ryan and on having an actual conversation with Chip Ackerson that I didn't even notice!

"Are you…are you going to use that in the wedding special?" I ask.

Chip gives me a winning smile. "We just might!" Then his cameraman waves him over, and he starts to walk away. But then he pauses for a second. "Hey, aren't you one of the teens who auditioned for *Pastry Wars* this season?"

I almost keel over. He remembers me! "Um, yeah. That was me. I made a mille-feuille." This time, I actually pronounce it correctly.

"That's right!" he says. "I knew you looked familiar." Then he lowers his voice. "Between you and me, you came really close to being chosen."

"Really?"

He nods. "We all thought you had a lot of potential, but it felt like you were trying too hard. You said you like to make up your own recipes, but then you made something we've seen tons of times before. When you audition again next year, make sure to do something that's really you, okay?"

I blink. "When I audition again?"

"You're not going to give up after one try, are you?" he says. Then he gives me his winning smile before he and the cameraman wander off to get some shots of the lake.

When I look back at Chef Ryan, I expect him to still be glaring at me. But instead, there's a strange look on his face, and it doesn't look nearly as murderous as it did before.

"Well," he says finally. "I can't say I'm happy about you ruining my cake."

"I know. I'm so sorry! I never meant to—"

"But what you have here is the best work I've ever seen you do. I'm glad you finally got your passion back." Then he flashes me what could actually pass for a smile and wheels back to the other side of the tent.

"Okay," Cherie says. "Let's put the cake toppers on here and get this in place. This wedding's about to start!"

Chapter 25

When the guests start arriving, everyone is obviously impressed with the location, the decorations, and my cake. I even see people taking pictures of it out of the corner of my eye as I help Briana and Cherie's daughters dish out the food. Cherie even tells me that she's glad to have me here helping, even if it means the bakery is closed for the day. I'm so excited about how everything's turned out that I don't even care that I have to spend the day passing out appetizers and stuff.

From what I can see, the ceremony goes off without a hitch. Ms. Montelle—Mrs. Brennan now—is glowing with happiness, and even Caitlin is beaming. Honestly, I think it's the first time I've seen her smile widely enough to show her teeth.

When the reception starts, guests begin pouring into the food tent, and I get my serving spoons ready to dish out pasta like a fiend. After a minute, I spot a familiar orange dress moving through the crowd. It's the one Marisol was making for Ms. Emerald! Sure enough, when I look more closely, I recognize the teacher standing near the bride and groom. I realize, suddenly, that she looks exactly like Mr. Brennan. Oh my goldfish. This must be the brother whose wedding she was going to! The dress Marisol made came out perfect, as usual. I don't know why I ever bothered doubting her skills.

"Hey," Briana says, snapping me back to reality. "Cherie asked me to go serve hors d'oeuvres to the wedding party, but I think you should do it."

"I'm pretty busy here."

"Please," she says, her eyes suddenly pleading. "I don't want…anyone to see me like this."

"Too late." I point to Caitlin who's staring at us from across the tent. I can tell Briana is tempted to dive behind a nearby table, but Caitlin is already on her way over.

"What are you doing here?" Caitlin asks. "I thought you said you were out of town this weekend so you couldn't come, and now you're hiding in the corner and won't even come talk to me?"

"Um, hello? I'm like a servant at your mom's wedding!"

Briana says. "You really want to come over and say hi when I'm, like, waiting on you? It's so embarrassing!"

"Is this why you've been so weird lately?" Caitlin asks.

Briana only looks at the floor.

"I can't believe you didn't tell me about your dad losing his job or about you working at the bakery. I had to find out from Angela Bareli! Now *that's* embarrassing. Why didn't you tell me the truth?"

Briana shrugs. "Because you'd think I was a total loser. Besides, you were so busy with the wedding that I didn't think you'd care."

"Are you crazy?" Caitlin says. "Of course I care! I mean, we've been best friends forever!"

"After everything that happened between us last year, I wasn't sure you still felt that way." For once Briana's voice is soft and hesitant.

"Don't be stupid," Caitlin says. "Next time you're dealing with stuff, tell me, okay? Then we can figure it out together." She pulls Briana into a big hug, and just like that, everything is okay between them again.

"What are you staring at?" Briana snaps at me, but her usual venom is gone. She's almost smiling as she gets back to work.

The Truth Game

As I keep dishing out pasta, I can't help thinking about how oddly similar my and Marisol's friendship is to Briana and Caitlin's. Okay, maybe we're not two semi-spoiled popular girls, but we've had our ups and downs too. And we've both been so busy with our own things recently that it's felt like we were on two different planets. But then I realize that Caitlin is a better friend than I am, because she offered to help Briana with the things she was dealing with, and all I've done is complain about how much the Fashion Club has been taking up Marisol's time. I never offered to help her get it started, and when she asked for my help, I totally blew her off. No wonder she's mad at me. I've been the worst friend.

But maybe it's not too late to fix things. After all, I'm almost as good at fixing mistakes as I am at making them.

I keep dishing out food all through dinner and then watch with a mixture of glee and awe as Mrs. Brennan and her new husband share bites of my cake in front of everyone. Then the cake gets rushed back to us, and Cherie and I cut it while Briana and the other two girls distribute it among the tables. Everyone oohs and aahs over the cake, which feels amazing, but I'm a little distracted with keeping track of Ms. Emerald and hoping she doesn't decide to leave early before I have a chance to talk to her.

Finally, when the cake is all distributed, I beg Cherie to take over my station for a second, and then I run over to catch Ms. Emerald as she's finishing signing the guest book.

"Hi, Ms. Emerald. You probably don't know me, but—"

"I heard you're the one who made the delicious cake!" she says. "It was so good that I snuck back for another piece! You are one talented young lady."

"Wow, thank you," I say.

"Are you in the Cooking Club at school?" she asks.

"Um, yeah," I say. "It's been kind of...different from what I thought. Actually, that's what I wanted to talk to you about."

"The Cooking Club?"

"No. The Fashion Club." Then I explain to her how Marisol has been practically killing herself trying to prove to Ms. Emerald that she deserves to have her own club. "I mean, your dress looks great. Isn't that proof enough?"

She laughs. "I have gotten lots of compliments on it. And I admire Marisol's tenacity, but I'm not sure I have the time to take on anything new. I've been put in charge of doing a complete overhaul of the school lunches for next year, and it's taking up all my time."

I almost laugh out loud. This has to be the pineapple

gods again, right? There's no way this is a coincidence. "The school lunches? I know the exact person you should talk to. And if you need some help coming up with new recipes, I'm happy to do it."

"When will you have time to do all of that?" Ms. Emerald asks. "I imagine the bakery keeps you pretty busy."

"It does," I say, "but if it means helping my best friend, I'll make the time."

"All right," Ms. Emerald says. "You have yourself a deal."

Chapter 26

The day after the wedding, I'm pretending to pack up my closet while still floating on a fluffy buttercream cloud when Mom pops her head into my room.

"Your dad is here," she says. "We wanted to talk to you."

I sit on my bed. "Why? What's wrong?"

"Nothing is wrong," she says. "But we thought it was time for us to sit down and have a family talk."

As I follow her out into the living room, my heart starts pounding in my chest. Last time we had a family meeting, my dad announced he was moving to Florida, and my entire life fell apart.

I find not only Dad but also Mr. Hammond sitting on the couch. Um, okay. I guess Mr. Hammond is part of our family meetings now. It makes sense, I guess, but it's still a little odd. Then again, maybe having him here will help keep my mom calm. We definitely don't want another shouting match like we had at Molly's.

"What's going on?" I ask.

"Your mom and I sat down and crunched some numbers yesterday," Dad says. "And we think we've come up with a solution for the living situation."

I swallow and sink down in an armchair, getting ready for bad news. Is Mom selling the house and Dad deciding to move to Australia or something?

"Now that I've finally found a job where I can see myself staying long-term," Dad continues, "I think it makes sense for me to buy out your mom's half of the house and live here."

I stare at him. "Say what?"

"That means that you'd get to keep your old room," Mom says, "and stay here whenever you want. Now that we're both in town, there's no reason you need to be with me all the time."

"You could even live here if you wanted and visit your mom and Robert," Dad adds.

Mom bites her lip, clearly a little upset at the idea, but she nods in support. "We think you're old enough to be involved in deciding this with us."

"So what do you think, Roo?" Dad asks. "Do you want to stay here and live with me?"

"Don't put her on the spot, Ted!" Mom says, but she doesn't sound angry.

"Um." I think about the old me from last year, the one who stole money to fly down to Florida to convince her dad to come home. She would have jumped at the chance to stay in this house and be with him. But so much has changed since then. Dad and I are still close, but being apart has made our relationship different. And thanks to all we've been through, Mom and I are closer than ever. I can't imagine not seeing her every day, but the idea of living with Mr. Hammond is also scary. Then again, I feel like all I do are scary things these days. From kissing Evan to climbing a rock wall to being on TV! Maybe doing scary things is part of who I am now. Maybe one day I might even learn how to not be scared of them anymore.

"I want to live with Mom and Mr. Ha—and Robert," I say slowly. "But if I could have my old room here, Dad, then I could stay with you whenever I wanted, couldn't I?"

"Anytime," he says. He seems a little sad, but he's smiling.

"Then I want to give it a try," I say. And even though

I'm kind of terrified at the idea of living somewhere new, I'm also excited.

"Excellent," Mom says. "But when you're on TV in a couple of weeks, we're watching it here, okay? It would feel wrong to do it anywhere else."

"I might not even be on TV. They might have cut me out of the episode or something!" I say, but I'm grinning. As long as my cake is in the show, that's all I need.

● ● ●

That night, Marisol shows up at my door holding my favorite shirt.

"I was looking for that!" I say. "Where did you find it? And why does it have sequins on it?" Then I realize the sequins are hiding a pretty hideous toothpaste stain.

Marisol laughs. "I stole it from your room right after school started to cover up the stain, since I know it's your favorite. Sorry it took me so long to get it back to you, but I guess I've been a little too wrapped up in my own stuff."

She holds it out to me, and I realize the sequins are in the shape of a piece of cake. "It's perfect. Thank you." I look at her. "So...how are you?"

Instead of answering, she pulls me into a huge hug. "Thank you!" she says in my ear. "Ms. Emerald told me what you did. You have no idea how much that means to me."

"It's the least I could do," I say as she finally lets me go. "I've been the worst friend, not just recently but for years. I always drag you into crazy stuff and make you listen to all my drama, and the one time you needed my help, I totally wasn't there."

She shakes her head. "I haven't been a great friend recently either. No wonder you didn't tell me about kissing Evan right away. I've barely been around! I don't blame you for wishing things were like they used to be."

"But they can't be, can they?" That's certainly something I learned the hard way when I was trying to get my family back together.

"No, but that doesn't mean they can't be good." She laughs. "I still don't know what you were thinking spilling my secrets on the Internet, but my mom and I had a serious talk yesterday, and she's finally coming around about this boyfriend thing. And thanks to you, Andrew's life is pretty good right now too. Ms. Emerald is going to have the school board watch his documentary. She thinks it'll help them see how much better the lunches can be."

"Wow, really?"

"You're invited to the screening, if you want to come." She lowers her voice to a whisper. "We might have to pray to the pineapple gods that we don't fall asleep during it."

"So you *do* remember!" I say. "I was afraid you forgot all about them."

She blushes. "I did at first, but then I prayed to them the other night, and the next day, I got a call from Ms. Emerald saying that my fashion club was a go and that I had you to thank. That can't be a coincidence, can it?"

"Definitely not," I say. "The pineapple gods never fail us." After all, my prayers came true too.

"Praise be to their delicious tropical juices," Marisol and I say in unison. Then we both erupt into giggles.

Just then, my phone beeps. Another Truth Game questionnaire, this one on embarrassing moments.

"Oh boy," I say. "I have plenty of those to share."

Marisol wrinkles her forehead. "You're still doing that game, even after everything?"

"No, I just haven't gotten around to deleting it yet. Honestly, it was fun to see how I measure up to people, at least at first. But then I thought—"

"That you don't care about that kind of stuff?" Marisol asks hopefully.

I roll my eyes. "I wish. No, I do care how I compare to others, but that doesn't mean I need to see it in number form. Like, if I hadn't rushed to kiss Evan because I was so paranoid about having never been kissed, I bet our first kiss wouldn't have involved gym shorts!"

Marisol laughs. "I'm sure you would have found some other way to mess it up," she jokes.

"I'm sure I would have," I say. "But then I would have fixed it."

Because that's what I do.

Chapter 27

The day after my big TV debut, Dad drops me off at school in the morning. I'm wearing my favorite shirt and actually kind of enjoying how the sequins Marisol put on it are glittering in the sun. My hair is pulled back into a high ponytail so that it actually shows my widow's peak. I figured instead of making my hair do things it's not made to do, I'll try working with what I have. I'm not sure I'm sold on the look yet, but maybe I need some time to get used to it.

"I'll pick you up after I get out of work this afternoon, okay?" Dad says.

I nod. "I hope I don't chicken out."

He laughs. "You already climbed that wall once. You'll be great."

Whoever thought that Rachel Lee, gym class disaster, would be looking forward to another rock-climbing session? But I'm actually excited to go back. "Okay, see you then," I say, hopping out of the car.

"Have a great day," Dad calls after me. "Oh, and your mom told me to remind you to floss after lunch!"

I hurry away, hoping no one heard him, and spot Angela hanging out with her cross-country friends by the flagpole.

She gives me a little wave and yells, "You were so awesome on TV last night! Your wedding cake rocked!"

"Thanks!" I call back, but I don't slow down to talk to her. I don't think I'll ever totally trust Angela after everything that's happened. She might seem like a different person, but there are things about ourselves that we can't change. Some we might not even want to.

When I get to my locker, the kissing couple is in front of it again. Gross.

"Excuse me," I say.

They don't budge.

"Hello?" I say.

Nothing.

Finally, I snap my fingers in front of their faces, and they break apart, looking seriously annoyed. "What do you want?" the girl asks.

"Wait," the guy says. "You were on that cooking show last night. You're, like, famous."

Wow. I had no idea so many people knew about the Cooking Channel special. Honestly, I was only in it for all of two minutes. They played a clip of me explaining my cake disaster—so embarrassing but actually pretty funny!—and then showed a couple shots of my cake and of people gobbling it up. It was better than I could have dreamed.

"Yup, that was me," I say.

"Nice," he says with something like respect on his face. Then he turns to the girl and says, "Come on. Let's go hang out at my locker. It's quieter there anyway."

And just like that, they're gone. I can't help grinning in triumph, and I'm still grinning when I run into Pierre outside the home ec room.

"Hey, Rachel," he says. "Great job on the show last night."

"Thanks," I say. "How did your sludge come out?"

He sighs. "Not good. I'm going to try a slurry next."

"Sounds…interesting."

"Have you thought of a goal for the year yet? I'm thinking I might try a different one, maybe something about gels instead of foams."

I shrug. With everything that's been going on, I haven't

had much time to think about it. I start to say "to get better at baking," but then I can almost hear Mrs. Da Silva telling me to make it more specific. So I say, "Maybe something about learning the basics. I know most of them already, but I want to know what I don't know, you know?"

Pierre gives me a confused look, but I don't bother explaining. It makes perfect sense to me.

I head to Marisol's locker—finally managing to navigate the endless identical hallways without getting lost—and find her having an animated conversation with Andrew. For once, he's the one doing all the talking. When I get closer, I realize he's going on and on about how much the school board loved his documentary.

"The principal is going to make the whole school watch it next week, all three hours of it. Isn't that great?" he says.

Marisol and I share a look, and it's like the past couple of weeks never happened. We're totally on the same wavelength again, even if we also have a lot of our own stuff going on now.

"Rachel!" I hear Evan call. I turn and see him walking toward me. For a second, the old panic comes back. Should I kiss him? Hug him? Give him a high five?

But then he's in front of me, grinning, and all that

goes out of my head. Because it doesn't matter if I get things perfect. Let's face it. Most of the time, I probably won't. But that doesn't mean I won't find a way to get them right eventually.

Acknowledgments

Thank you to all the young readers who asked for a fourth book—you inspired me to keep telling Rachel's story. My thanks to Aubrey Poole for being open to the idea of adding one more volume to the Dirt Diary "trilogy," to Ammi-Joan Paquette for helping me get this story right, to Sarah Chessman for her culinary wisdom, to my family for the endless support, and to Ray Brierly for always being excited to read the next book.

About the Author

Anna Staniszewski lives outside Boston and teaches at Simmons College. She was a writer-in-residence at the Boston Public Library and a winner of the PEN New England Discovery Award. When she's not writing, Anna reads as much as she can, eats lots of chocolate, and avoids cleaning her house. Visit her at www.annastan.com.

The Dirt Diary

EIGHTH GRADE NEVER SMELLED SO BAD.

Rachel Lee didn't think anything could be worse than her parents splitting up. She was wrong. Working for her mom's new house-cleaning business puts Rachel in the dirty bathrooms of the most popular kids in the eighth grade. Which does not help her already loser-ish reputation. But her new job has surprising perks: enough dirt on the in-crowd to fill up her (until recently) boring diary. She never intended to reveal her secrets, but when the hottest guy in school pays her to spy on his girlfriend, Rachel decides to get her hands dirty.

The Prank List

TO SAVE HER MOM'S CLEANING BUSINESS, RACHEL'S ABOUT TO GET HER HANDS DIRTY—AGAIN.

Rachel Lee is having the best summer ever taking a baking class and flirting with her almost-sort-of-boyfriend Evan— until a rival cleaning business swoops into town, stealing her mom's clients. Rachel never thought she'd fight for the right to clean toilets, but she has to save her mom's business. Nothing can distract her from her mission...except maybe Whit, the cute new guy in cooking class. Then she discovers something about Whit that could change everything. After destroying her Dirt Diary, Rachel thought she was done with secrets, but to save her family's business, Rachel's going to have to get her hands dirty. Again.

The Gossip File

SOME THINGS ARE BEST KEPT SECRET...

Rachel is spending the holiday break with her dad and soon-to-be step-monster, Ellie. Thank goodness her BFF Marisol gets to come with. But when Rachel meets a new group of kids and realizes she can leave her loser status back home, quirky Marisol gets left behind. Bored and abandoned, Marisol starts a Gossip File, collecting info on the locals. When the gossip includes some dirt on Ellie, Rachel has to decide if getting the truth is worth risking her new cool-girl persona...